"Where's Daddy?"

"Where's Daddy?"

by William Roos

Doubleday & Company, Inc., Garden City, New York,

All of the characters in this book are fictitious,
and any resemblance to actual persons, living or dead,
is purely coincidental.

For Audrey

"Where's Daddy?"

Chapter One

"Hello, Ed," I said.

"Thank you," Ed said, "for letting us visit you this evening."

"That's all right," I said. "We weren't going anywhere."

"Who's that sitting on your right? Anyone you know?"

"That's Tom, my husband."

"Hello, Tom!"

"Hello, Ed," Tom said.

"And who's that young man on your left?"

"Our son," I said. "Gordy."

"Hello, Gordy," Ed said. "How old are you?"

"Ten. Are we on television now? Right this minute, I mean?"

"That you are," Ed said. "How does it feel?"

"Not any different," Gordy said.

"That's a lovely room, Mrs. Wade. Charming."

"This old thing," I said.

"Just how old is your house?"

"It's about 1780, we think."

"I found a 1936 penny in the cellar," Gordy said, "so it's at least that old for sure."

"Have you always lived in Connecticut?"

"I have," Gordy said, "they haven't. Am I talking too much?"

"Yes," I said.

"I thought so."

Ed said, "You must be very proud, Tom, of your charming wife and that fine boy. And I'm sure they're just as proud of you. How about it, Gordy?"

Gordy squirmed. Desperately, he turned to me. "Isn't it time I was in bed?"

Ed laughed. "Tom . . . do you commute?"

"Where to?" Tom asked.

"Well," Ed said, lighting another cigarette, "New York?"

"No," Tom said.

"Oh," Ed said, lighting another cigarette. "But you do commute?"

"No," Tom said.

"Lucky fellow. What do you do?"

Gordy said, "Don't tell him, Daddy!"

"Ed," I said quickly, "wouldn't you like to see the rest of the house?"

"In a moment, thanks. Tom, tell me, what do you do?"

"Mommy!" Gordy yelled. "Don't let him!"

"Ed, you must see the rest of the house!"

I rose, tripped over wires as I hurried to the living room door. I opened it. There was no rest of our house. It was gone. Going, rather. I could still see the man taking it away . . .

I woke up screaming.

Chapter Two

The day it all began dawned like any other day. There the resemblance ended. First, we got up in plenty of time; that alone should have tipped me off. Then Tom and Gordy found all their clothes by themselves. There wasn't a single button off any of them. The three of us sat down to breakfast simultaneously, smiling. We had time to talk.

"It's the bottom of the ninth," Gordy said. "Tie score, two out, no one on base. I'm up. The crowd's going wild. I dig in."

"I drop the resin bag," Tom said. "I step onto the mound, look you over. I get my sign. I wind up. I make the pitch."

"I let it go," Gordy said.

"Strike one!" I said.

"Nice call," Tom said.

"Robber!" Gordy said. "You're blind!"

"Play ball," I said coldly.

"I wind up," Tom said. "I'm cool as a cucumber. I make the pitch."

"I dig in," Gordy said. "I'm like ice. I swing. I get ahold of it! It streaks for the left field bleachers. It's going, going, gone! The crowd goes nuts. I trot around the bases . . ."

"Foul ball," I said.

"What! Mom, you need glasses, you . . ."

"Game called," I said. "On account of school bus."

Gordy got on the bus without denouncing compulsory education. Tom didn't have to rush to catch his train. He had time to kiss me good-by, so much time that for a moment it looked as if he might miss his train.

I should have realized when I took the laundry out of the

dryer what was happening. I came up with an even number of socks. When I went marketing I remembered to take the empty bottles back, even the one that had been on the garage window sill for two years. When I got the mail there were no depressing, vital messages to Occupant or Householder reminding me that our roof needed attention, our lawn sprayed, our termites eliminated. There were only two happy, newsy letters from old friends and a credit of thirty-two dollars and nine cents for a Bloomingdale bill that Tom, bless him, had paid twice.

It had gone on like that all day. It didn't dawn on me until the ice tray didn't stick when I got the cocktail tray ready that I, like Gordy when he's pitching in the Family League, had a perfect day going.

If this kept up I would probably be the first wife and mother who had ever pitched a perfect day. It would be a break-through; I would be an inspiration. Sometime, somewhere, a wife and mother would pitch a perfect week, a perfect month. Utopia would no longer be a dream, at least not around the house.

Now, like in baseball, when the crowd holds its breath on every pitch, I held mine when I reached for the vermouth bottle. There wouldn't be enough. There often wasn't. I don't know why I can keep enough of everything on hand except dry vermouth. With Grandmother it was Scott's Emulsion, with my mother it was Ovaltine, with me vermouth. This evening there was plenty.

I carried the cocktail things into the living room; the room looked charming. The evening sun, slanting through the window, didn't illuminate a single cobweb. There were no clothes, books, hockey sticks, pucks, basketball bladders, nor anything dead on the floor.

Then another miracle. Tom tooted his horn in the driveway. For the third consecutive evening the New Haven Railroad had run Tom's train on time. There he was, standing in the doorway, relaxed and happy. His day in the rat race had left him unmarked. There was no new gray in his hair, no new lines on his face, no new droop to his shoulders. He wasn't even twitching. He was smiling. And that wasn't all.

"Darling!" I said. "Flowers! For me?"

"Sure." He kissed me. "I like your hair that way. Dinner smells good."

"I haven't started it yet."

"Oh. Maybe it's you. Where's Gordy?"

"Upstairs. Doing his homework."

"Damn grind." Tom went out into the hall. "Hey, Gordy! I got you that Stutz Bearcat model!"

There was thunder on the stairs. The men conferred happily over the gift, Tom proving it is more blessed to give, Gordy proving, even more conclusively, it is more blessed to receive.

I poured the martinis. Tom tasted his; I waited anxiously.

"Perfect," he said.

"Darling," I said.

"Em," Tom said, "there's something I want to talk to you about."

"Anything, dear, anything."

"You don't seem to be really listening."

"I am now. Go on, dear."

"You seem strange, excited . . ."

I couldn't tell Tom what was going on. That would certainly jinx it. Like in baseball, nobody breathes a word about the no-hitter until the last out of the last inning. I couldn't breathe a word to Tom until the last stroke of midnight.

"Tom, I'm fine. You were saying?"

"Yeah . . . how shall I say it? Em . . ."

"You sound so serious!"

Tom nodded. "I am serious. Em, you've always taken for granted that we were happy, you and I. That we've both been happy . . ."

"Haven't we been?" I heard myself saying. "I have. Haven't you?"

"Well," Tom said, "no."

There it was. There went the ball game. My perfect day was ruined. Not by the chops burning, or a drain choking up, or the roof caving in. Just by my husband telling me that we weren't happy. He wasn't, that is.

"Who is she?" I asked.

"What?"

"Who's the lucky girl?"

"Em, will you not say anything? Let me explain and try to understand. Want another drink?"

"No. Please, Tom, go ahead."

"Well . . ."

"Clear your throat."

He did. "Well . . ."

"That's better."

"Thanks. Em, I never meant for things to end up for me this way. Somehow it seems as though I didn't have anything to do with it. It was all decided for me . . . by circumstances beyond my control or other people. I didn't ever want to live like this . . . if you can call this living."

I didn't say anything; I just tried to understand.

"I've been going on year after year . . . the model husband and father, the happy provider. And all the time I've been dying! Dying, Em. Well, this is the end. This is where I'm getting off. I've had it. This may knock you for a loop. I don't blame you and I'm sorry, Em, but I've quit my job."

I said, "You've what?"

"Quit my job."

"That's all?"

"Yes, what did you . . ."

"Tom! You darling!"

"You don't mind?"

"Oh, Tom!"

"Yeah! No more commuting, no more Madison Avenue, no more writing nauseating, moronic advertising copy. No more worrying what any copy chiefs, account executives, vice presidents, clients, anyone upstairs, downstairs, in Chicago, on the Coast, at NBC, ABC, CBS, or their affiliates think about me. No more . . ."

"Wait a minute," I said slowly.

"What, Em?"

"You quit your job?"

"Yes!"

"Do you mean to stand there and tell me that you've quit your job?"

"Em, what's the matter with you?"

"You've got another job. Of course! Not in advertising, something different . . ."

"No! I'm never going to work in an office as long as I live. Never again will I worry about a raise, a promotion or getting fired. I may never even ride the New Haven Railroad again. Not even on Sundays or holidays. No more . . ."

"Wait a minute," I said slowly.

"Now what?"

"No more salaries . . . ever again?"

"Not so long as I live."

"You're going to earn money some other way."

"Right! By doing what I've wanted to do all my life."

"There's something you've wanted to do all your life . . . and I don't know about it?"

"I've never told anyone."

"Oh, Lord . . . are you ever going to? Can you?"

"I'm going to be a writer. Novels."

"A writer. Novels. Well, why all the secrecy all these years? Are you going to write dirty books?"

Tom laughed. "I'm glad to see you're taking this so well."

"I don't think I'm taking it so well. Have you started a novel?"

"No."

"Have you an idea for a novel?"

"Millions of them!"

"Yes, but do you have one?"

"I'm going to mix another batch of martinis."

"Where did that batch all go?"

"You drank most of it."

"See, I'm not taking this so well."

"Be right back."

"Wait. Look, Tom, I have every confidence in you, but what in God's name makes you think you can write a novel all of a sudden? I think, coming from the penniless mother of your unemployed child, that is a very fair question."

"I've just got a feeling. I've always had it."

"I think," I said, "you'd better mix another batch of martinis."

"Look, you're not worried?"

"Me? What about?"

"That's the girl!"

I sat there trying not to remember how much money we had in the bank, the size of our mortgage, and sundry other financial details. I firmly closed from my mind all tales of writers starving for years in garrets, their wives selling matches, their children sweeping chimneys. This was the end of my perfect day.

Tom came out of the kitchen. He wore a bereaved look around his eyes like a pair of dark glasses. His voice was reproachful.

"The vermouth is all gone."

"Of course," I said. "I'm not surprised."

"No vermouth," Tom said. "Well, let's go out, celebrate! Have a couple more drinks and dinner . . . hey, it's raining!"

"Pouring!" I said.

Gordy yelled from upstairs. "The roof's leaking up here! Like everything!"

"Naturally," I called back cheerfully.

Chapter Three

The alarm rang at quarter of seven and before I came to, Tom had struggled out of bed and stumbled into the bathroom. By the time I caught up with him he had his face half lathered.

"Darling, wake up!" I said. "Don't you remember?"

"Huh?"

"No train to catch. You quit."

"Yeah . . . I quit!"

"Yes."

"I really did, didn't I?"

"Yes."

"Lindstrom! You should have seen Lindstrom, the look on his face! I've waited for that moment for years. I've dreamed about it, rehearsed it . . ."

"Can't we discuss this quietly over a cup of coffee?"

"Lindstrom never had anyone quit before. He strikes first. But I outmaneuvered him. He hadn't an inkling when I walked into his office. He thought I wanted a raise and he was all set to give it to me . . . a raise and a vice presidency . . ."

"Please, Tom, I don't want to hear any more. A raise."

"And then I let him have it. You ever see anyone livid, really livid? It's a color and on Lindstrom it looks simply wonderful. It's his color. He took four different kinds of pills and sent out for some yoghurt. When I left him his nose was beginning to bleed . . ."

"A raise," I said. "Oh, well, you're happy. Look, why don't you go back to bed? Your first morning . . . sleep till all hours, celebrate."

"I want to see Gordy off to school. I can do that now."

"Your first morning . . . he'll understand."

"Sure," Gordy yelled from his room. "I'll understand. Go back to bed, live it up."

"Say," Tom said, "Gordy shouldn't have to go to school today, not today of all days."

"Now, now," Mother said. "Let's not overdo it. Go back to bed."

"Back to bed," Tom said in awe. "Thursday and I'm going back to bed. Come and watch me. Hey, Gordy, come and watch me go back to bed."

"Gee, thanks! Hey, Mom, where's my camera?"

"Look underneath things. But let's not miss the bus."

The school bus stops in front of our house. No one Gordy's age boards it here and, since he considers any junior citizen not his age a drip, regardless of race, color, or creed, he seldom joins the gathering. It's our ritual, when we get up early enough, to wait together in the hall and watch the kids until the bus arrives. It's consistently worth while. Those kids don't just stand there.

There are the usual, unimaginative pinchers and hair-pullers to keep things humming generally. Then Timmy Lenhardt and Jim Costigan, each weighing in at about eighty-five pounds, are almost certain to trade blows. They're very evenly matched and there aren't those constant, nagging beer commercials.

Gordy likes it best when Francine Kimberly drops her books. He bets me a nickel every morning that she will, and his weekly winnings from me average about twenty cents. In the long run it would be cheaper for me to buy Francine a briefcase.

Personally, for early morning programing, I like the currying and grooming of the Talbots best. Milly and Bob Talbot have four girls, all of them between the ages of fourteen and nine. They are lovely girls. I wouldn't mind having one or two of them myself, except that somehow they haven't yet grasped the concept of looking presentable. They seem to find it impossible to even lift a finger toward that end.

Milly carts them down Pudding Hill Lane in a station wagon. She makes them all sit in back so that she can keep checking them in the rear-view mirror. At the stop she jumps out first, opens the back door, or floodgate, allows one girl to come out, quickly closes the floodgate. She inspects number one, sighs, and pitches in . . . always with comb, brush, and Kleenex, often with the needle and thread she wears in the lapel of her school bus coat. This coat is fully equipped to meet any emergency. She yanks and pulls at garments, making them momentarily fit. She replaces all soiled Band-Aids. Four times she works her way down a daughter in crescendo of hysterical despair as the bus's arrival crowds in on her. The final Talbot girl is always last on the bus, with Milly working on her from behind until the door closes.

Then Milly drags herself back under her steering wheel, looks for a moment as if she's going to crash full speed into the stone wall across the road, shakes herself, and heads for home. If she isn't a secret drinker, I more than admire her. At least a few good stiff belts every morning just when the school bells start ringing.

"There go Francine's books," Gordy said. "You owe me another nickel."

"Right," I said. "Here come the Talbots. Say, there's something different about them today."

"I don't see anything."

"Oh, yes. Gwen got a new coat and three old ones moved down a notch. Well, Tom!"

"Can't you sleep, Pop?"

"No, it's all too wonderful!"

"That's the way it is," Gordy said. "When you can sleep, you can't, when you can't, you can."

"Invariably," Tom said.

"It beats everything," Gordy said.

Tom put one arm around Gordy, the other around me, but he didn't watch the kids waiting for the bus. He watched the cars, headed for the station, stream by.

"Jim Carey," he said. "That's the cigarette he lit to have with his coffee. Here comes Max Wendell, talking to himself . . . Sam McKee, using his electric razor." Tom's smile became a running chuckle. "Look at them! The poor bast . . . the poor guys. I ought to go down to the station and see them off, cheer them on. Except I might get lynched. Here's Fred Downing . . . look, he's sore already, bawling out Clara . . . brother, look at them! I don't know how lucky I am."

"What's the name of your book going to be, Daddy?"

"A title, yes! I've got to have a good one, that's important. I'm glad you brought it up, partner."

"I'll help all I can," Gordy promised.

"You coming right home after school?" Tom asked.

"Why?"

"I thought we might shoot a few baskets."

"Okay! Say, this is great . . . you being a writer."

"Here comes the bus," I said.

"So long, Gordy," Tom said. "Give them hell today on Woodchuck Lane."

"So long, Pop, give them hell today on Madison . . . hey, I can't say that anymore!"

"Praise the Lord," Tom said. "You got plenty of money?"

"What for?" Gordy asked.

"A fellow ought to carry a little money. No more than he can afford to lose, of course. Where's my wallet? Gordy, look in the television room closet . . . my gray jacket. I'll look upstairs."

"Hurry," I said.

My boys shot off in different directions. Gordy was back first. He yelled up to Tom, "I've got your wallet but it's empty. Should I take one of your credit cards?"

Tom came running down. "No, I found five dollars."

"Five dollars!" Gordy said.

"Five dollars!" I said.

"It'll have to do," Tom said.

"Thanks! Gee!"

"So long, kid. Give them hell on Woodchuck Lane."

"There goes the bus," I said.

"Yeah," Gordy said. "I missed the bus."

"Yeah," Tom said. "You did, didn't you?"

"But it's all right," Gordy said. "I can afford to take a taxi."

"I'll drive you," Tom said.

Tom laughed.

"Eat your breakfast, dear."

"I don't know how lucky I am."

"Eat your breakfast, dear."

"They're getting off the train now, pushing and shoving their way up the ramp like cattle on their way to slaughter. Or maybe the train broke down in the tunnel. The air conditioning is out. Their heads are beginning to throb, their stomachs burn. They are trying each other's pills . . . I don't know how lucky I am."

"More coffee, dear?"

The phone rang; Tom answered it.

"Hello. Hello, Milly, it's me, Tom. No, I'm not sick. In fact, I never felt better in my life. I quit my job, Milly. I said I quit my job. No, no, it was voluntary. I'm a writer now, Milly. A writer. Writer . . . author. You know, books. Salinger, John O'Hara. No, Milly, they aren't here. I meant they're writers, too, I was just trying to explain. No, Milly, I'm not sick. I'm not hiding anything from you. Of course I don't mind your being blunt with me. Of course we're old friends. Milly, I swear if I had something incurable you and

Bob would be the first to know. I'd have wired you from New York."

Tom's voice rose.

"Milly, I'm home because I'm going to be a writer."

His voice tightened.

"Yes, I do think I can be a writer just like that. Writers are born, not made. What? I was born in Erie, Pennsylvania. What's that got to do with it, for God's sake?"

His voice became firm

"I am going to write a novel. No, I don't have a publisher. I don't even have a novel yet. Milly, the reason I'm standing here talking to you is because the phone rang and I answered it. I'm going to start writing any day now. Yes, of course Emmy knows. I told her first thing. Why, she seems to be taking it all right. What do you mean? Of course she's able to come to the phone . . ."

He turned to me. "She wants to talk to you. She's crying." He handed me the phone. "Dammit to hell! The idiot!"

"Hello, Milly," I said.

"You poor thing," Milly moaned. "I'm coming right over. Is there anything I can do?"

"No, Milly, please . . ."

"Can I take Gordy for a few days?"

"No, of course not."

"Did he actually quit? Deliberately?"

"Yes."

"He kept talking about being a writer."

"That's the idea, yes."

"Try not to be too upset. He may get over it."

"I don't want him to get over it," I said. "I'm in favor of it."

"That's right. Humor him. I remember when Carl Miller . . . you know Hilda and Carl, don't you? He's in communications? She's dumpy?"

"Yes."

"He wanted to raise mushrooms. Give up everything and raise mushrooms. Because they were so quiet, he said. But he got over it. Hilda pulled him out of it."

"I don't know if I'm dumpy enough."

"What, dear?"

"Nothing, I . . ."

"I understand. He's there, isn't he? Listening. You can't talk now."

"That's it."

"I thought so. Call me when he goes down cellar or someplace."

"All right."

" 'Bye, now. Oh, the reason I called. Might you be interested in the matinee on Saturday at New Haven? Helen Hayes and Rip Torn. Oh, no, of course not! You're not in any mood to enjoy a play, are you? My dear, if there's anything I can do, anything . . . and I promise not to tell a soul about this. Except Bob, of course. I do think he should know. 'Bye, now. Call the minute you can."

"Good-by, Milly, and thanks."

Tom was standing at the kitchen door. His hands, at his sides, were clenched.

"Are Salinger and O'Hara here, for God's sake!"

I accosted him gently. "Darling," I said, "don't mind Milly."

"Where was I born, for God's sake!"

"I think," I said, "for the next few days I'd better answer the phone."

Chapter Four

Last fall when Mother was visiting us she sat me down just before she left and said, "You know, dear, I've always tried to be impartial with you children. Your father made a point of that, if you can remember, and I've tried to do the same. I've never favored one over the others. But I must say, and I'm sure your father would forgive me, that I'd much rather visit with you than with Louise or Ed or Charles or Betsy. You have the loveliest guest room."

Tom's mother always says at least once as she looks around the room, "I could stay here forever. Just beautiful and so comfortable. Isn't it, George?" Tom's father is always certain to answer admiringly, "Beats staying in a hotel any day."

Lucy Carey, who turned to interior decoration when her husband turned to a younger woman who didn't talk so much, once said, while dropping ashes on our guest room floor, "Darling, you don't have to worry about Tom leaving you. You can come right into the shop with me. You have the touch, a divine room. And you obviously did it very cheaply."

Milly Talbot once said, "It's too good for guests." Mrs. Sill, our cleaning woman, often says, "A treat to clean." Sally Randall, an actress friend of ours, said, "It's a damn shame to have to sleep alone in a room like this." Saul McArdle, a college friend of Tom's, who now reviews books for a Titusville, Pennsylvania, newspaper, said, "Engrossing from start to finish. Enthralling. Kept me awake all night."

I, too, love and admire our guest room.

Tom Wade, my husband, who until yesterday held a lucrative position with a New York advertising firm, stood in the center of our guest room and said, "I have to have someplace to write."

I nodded numbly.

"Sweetheart! Look at it this way. You aren't losing a guest room, you're gaining a study."

I smiled wanly.

"Wait till you see what I do with it!"

I shuddered violently.

"This is going to be fun, Em, this room has possibilities. I'm beginning to see them." Tom measured the room with his eyes. I closed mine. "Of course I'll have to move things around a little to get a desk in."

"Um-hum."

"The beds can't be together like that. I'll shove that one against that wall, the other one against that wall." He pursed his lips judiciously. I bit mine. "I'll build a thing into the corner between the heads of the beds and put a . . . let's see . . . yes, a formica top on it."

"Formica."

"And a leather lamp on it."

"Leather."

"We'll get rid of those chintz bedspreads. We'll get corduroy."

"Corduroy."

"Maybe burlap curtains instead of all that gauze."

"Burlap."

"What's wrong?"

"Formica. Leather. Corduroy. Burlap. You go right ahead, Tom. You have to have someplace to write."

"Well, I do, don't I?"

"I admitted that you did."

"It'll be great," Tom said. "Masculine."

"Sweaty."

"Em, listen . . ."

"I have to take out a washing. Excuse me."

"Look, I'll start right in . . . if you're sure you don't mind."

"What makes you think I mind? These few tears?"

"Darling, if I'm going to be a writer, we all have to give up something."

"Of course. You gave up your job."

Tom chuckled. "The look on Lindstrom's face . . ."

"Please," I said, "no."

He glanced at his watch. "About now they're sending out for black coffee to get them through the morning . . ."

On my way to the cellar I stopped off in the kitchen and had a cup of black coffee. I could hear the scrape of moving furniture over my head and the voice of Tom raised in song. He was happy, and what are formica, leather, corduroy and burlap compared to a man's happiness? I could answer that one. They are, in alphabetical order, burlap, corduroy, formica, and leather.

Charley Everts came to the door with a package too big for our mailbox. There isn't, I bet, a more scrupulous postman on any route, urban or rural, in the U.S.A. We get a Christmas card every year from Charley and, although he delivers it himself, it always has a cancelled stamp.

Tom opened the door.

"Hiya, Charley! How's the boy?"

"Why, hello, there, Mr. Wade!" Charley was surprised to see Tom. "You're not at work today. Off your feed?"

"Nope!" Tom was beaming. "Never felt better in my life. Quit my job, Charley. No more rat race for me. I'm a writer now."

"A writer," Charley said.

"You said it, Charley!"

"How are you, Mrs. Wade?"

"Quite well, thank you, Charley."

"A writer," Charley said.

"That's right! Books, novels!"

"Books," Charley said. "Novels. I know what you mean. How's the boy, Mrs. Wade?"

"Fine, thanks."

"My wife belongs to the Book-of-the-Month Club, has for the past year. I haven't joined myself yet. So long for now."

Charley pulled the door shut behind him.

Tom watched him cross the lawn, climb back on his truck.

"I wonder," he said, "who reads the names and addresses on the mail for that guy. His wife belongs but he hasn't joined himself yet, for God's sake. What are you smiling about?"

"I didn't know I was. Darling, you can't expect everybody to jump up and down and clap their hands because you're a writer now."

"I've always been damned pleased about Charley being a mailman."

Al used to drive for Antoine Dry Cleaning and Laundry. In-Before-Nine, Out-Before-Six. When he left them to found Community Cleaners, In-Before-Ten, Out-Before-Five, naturally we went with him. Actually it's more often Out-Before-Five-Thirty or Quarter-to-Six. Al does his own picking up and delivering, which I find very satisfactory. When it's a question of a missing button or bow, it's good to be dealing directly with the head of the firm.

Al's a great conversationalist. If he spends as much time yakking in other kitchens as he does in mine, I have no idea what time he gets home to the little woman at night, hoarse. Take any subject, Al can be fluently at ease with it. He's very well versed and proud of it. I owe all I know about making fresh water out of oceans, desalination, that is, to Al.

"Well, Mr. Wade, I presume," Al said. "You're home today."

"Yes," Tom said.

"Under the weather?"

Tom glanced at me. "No," he said.

"Just taking the day off?"

"No," Tom said.

Al put the package of shirts on the table, hung Tom's gabardine suit on the dining room door frame. He brushed a bit of lint from its lapel, set its shoulders on the hanger so it was beautifully draped, a perfect fit.

"Miss your train?"

"No," Tom said.

"Oh," Al said, his voice solemn, "you're probably going to the funeral."

"No," Tom said, "I'm not going to any funeral."

I said, "Who died, Al?"

"Old Mrs. Keeley over on Songbird Lane. You didn't know her, Mrs. Wade?"

I shook my head. "No, I never did."

"Well, it's too late now." He turned back to Tom. "Stay home to donate some blood?"

"No," Tom said.

"Mr. Wade quit his job, Al," I said.

"That so?" Al turned back to Tom. "Retired?"

"No," Tom said.

"Mr. Wade," I said, "is going to be a writer."

"That so?" Al turned back to Tom. "That so, Mr. Wade? On the level? A writer?"

"Yes," Tom said defiantly. "A writer."

"Well," Al said. He took a deep breath and let it out in a dismal sigh. "Oh, boy," he said. "Oh, boy, oh, boy, oh, boy!"

"Yes?" Tom said quietly.

"Well, what's been done's been done, but let's look at it. You've been averaging five, six shirts a week, the gabardine there . . . incidentally, a beautiful piece of work, a pleasure to service . . . the gabardine one week, your gray weave the next, plus an occasional pair of slacks and jackets. I think you'll verify that, Mrs. Wade."

"I do, Al. Continue."

"Well, now you're a writer, Mr. Wade. I'll tell you how things will shape up. I've got other writers. You'll average about three, four shirts a month, the occasional pair of slacks and jackets occasionally. I'll be lucky if I see that gabardine and the gray weave two, three times a year."

"I'm sorry, Al," Tom said.

"Writers wear T-shirts, sport shirts, sweat shirts, washable pants," Al grieved. "Stuff their wives can throw in the washer. You don't make the regular weekly call on writers. So, Mrs. Wade, I won't be seeing you. I'll be out on the truck most likely when you drop the occasionals off at the shop. Well, good luck and good-by."

"Good-by, Al," I said.

"Good-by." Al turned toward the door, then back again. He seemed to be taking a last look at something. For a minute I didn't realize what it was. "And I'll miss that gabardine."

Sadly, he closed the door behind him.

"I'm sorry," Tom said, "to break up your beautiful friendship. Maybe he'll let you ride around on the truck with him once in a while, for God's sake. Oh, boy, oh, boy, oh, boy, for God's sake . . ."

"Tom, here comes the school bus. Why don't you meet Gordy?"

"Yeah," Tom said, "I'll meet Gordy."

Tom left the door wide open. I got to it in time to see Danny Hiller, the bus driver, lean out over the cascading kids to greet Tom.

"Hiya, Mr. Wade!" Danny said. "You didn't go to the office today?"

"I'm sick, Danny," Tom said. "Off my feed. Under the weather. Come on, Gordy."

Chapter Five

"Emmy . . ."

"Yes?"

"I hope you like it."

"But I will, Tom!" I said, as loudly as I could. "I will!"

"Understand it's only a mock-up, sort of . . ."

"Of course! You've only had one day."

"I tried to please you, too, Em. I know how you feel about your guest room . . ."

"Don't worry about that."

"But . . . well, shall we go in?"

I saw immediately how much I meant to Tom; he had really tried to please me. There wasn't a smidgeon of leather, formica, burlap, or corduroy in the place. The curtains, obviously hung only temporarily, were of pool table felt. On top of the thing he had built just for now between the beds was a slice of cork. On it was a lamp, shadeless yet, made out of a World War I shell. The covers of the beds, now looking like studio couches, were of something that looked like old awning.

The desk was a pair of two-drawer steel filing cabinets with a huge, unfinished flush door balanced on top of them. The filing cabinets were barely in sight of each other, making the knee-hole more than ample, you might say. The secondhand office swivel chair, with a new salmon-colored rubber pad on its seat, looked lonely.

"Nice, big desk, isn't it?" Tom said.

"You could land a Piper Cub on it."

"It won't look so big when I cover it," Tom said.

"With what?" I asked.

"A new thing I ordered. Silican. Well, Em, what do you think of it? The general effect?"

I nodded vigorously. "Yes!" I said. "Oh, yes! You've done it, Tom!"

"It's an office," Tom said, "you know."

"Yes! You certainly will be able to work here."

"I can't wait to get started. Notice those bedspreads? They won't wrinkle."

"They don't look as though they'd even fold."

A car ground gravel in our driveway.

"Damn," Tom said. "Who's that?"

"I'll see," I said.

"Get rid of them," Tom said.

I met Bob Talbot in the living room. He was panting. "Milly just told me," he said. "I came right over."

"You needn't have rushed so . . ."

"Where is he?"

"Upstairs. I'll call him."

"Just a moment, Emmy."

Bob put his hands on my shoulders, poured comfort into me from them and his clear, blue eyes. He smelled of Trim, the professional football players' perfume. He always smells of Trim; he must carry a flask of it on his hip. For years he smelled of Aqua Velva, until his agency lost that account.

His clear, red face smiled sadly but sympathetically down into mine. Bob is one of those sun worshipers who never tans. But every uncloudy Saturday and Sunday morning he goes up on the roof of their ranch-type house with yards of aluminum foil (an account of theirs) and makes his face beetred. With his red face, beautiful, wavy, white hair and blue eyes, one of his great-great-great grandmothers just had to be Betsy Ross.

"Emmy," he said, so earnestly I almost sobbed, "try not to worry. We'll lick this."

"Thanks, Bob."

"You know I always think of Tom . . . well, almost like a kid brother. We'll lick this."

"Thanks, Bob."

"All right. Get him down."

I went out into the hall and called upstairs. "Tom! Bob Talbot's here!"

"Tell him to come up."

"You'd better come down."

"I want to show him my office."

"I think, Tom, you had better come down."

"Okay."

I went back into the living room. Our flag was still there.

"Emmy," Bob said, "you didn't have any inkling of this? You didn't see it building?"

"No, it was all a surprise to me."

"I thought so. I'd like to think you'd have come to Milly and me. We might have nipped it in the bud . . . shh, he's coming."

Bob patted me so reassuringly on the shoulder that it hurt. Then he took a step forward, faced the hall door squarely, balancing lightly on the balls of his feet, his stance open. He seemed to spit on his hands, tighten his belt. He was calm, a little smile on his face, confident, eager. He was ready for Tom, ready to lick this thing.

Gordy walked in.

"Good evening, Mr. Talbot," he said.

"Hello, Gordy. Where's your father?"

"He's coming. How's Mrs. Talbot?"

"Fine, thanks."

"How's Gwen?"

"Fine."

"How's Sue?"

"Fine, fine."

"How's Polly?"

"Fine, they're all fine," Bob said impatiently. "You saw them all at school today, didn't you?"

"Yes," Gordy said. "They were all fine."

Bob glanced at his self-winding, waterproof, anti magnetic, calendar alarm wrist watch. "Gordy, will you call Mrs. Talbot and tell her I'll be a few minutes later than I expected."

"Yes, sir."

Gordy went on his errand. Tom walked in before Bob had a chance to get back on the balls of his feet.

"Hi, Bob," he said. "Want a drink?"

"Hello, there, Tom, hi, fella!"

"Want a drink?"

"No, thanks. I had my one in the club car."

Tom's face brightened. "Club car jammed? Stuffy? Train late?"

"A few minutes. Tom, boy . . ."

"Have to stand all the way to Norwalk?"

"Just Darien. Tom, Milly told me the news . . ."

"How is Milly?"

"Fine, thanks. Tom . . ."

"And Gwen?"

"The same. Listen, boy . . ."

"And Sue and . . ."

"Ask Gordy, damn it! Tom, I'm a bit hurt, Milly and I are both a bit hurt. You've always come to me for advice."

"Well, yes . . . or you've come over here."

"And I've given you good advice. Sound."

"Yes, you have, Bob. For instance, I've never regretted buying that lawn mower from you."

"But in a thing like this . . . throwing up everything, you use your own snap judgment."

"I've thought about it for years."

"No, you couldn't have . . . and made the decision you did. To throw up everything. Tom, boy, I'm quite a bit older than you . . ."

"Not that much."

"Yes, I am." Bob grinned his most boyish grin. "Appearances can be deceiving. Tom, I've watched you grow up on the Avenue. That you were with another agency didn't matter. We're all in the same league, different teams but the same league, and the league is only as strong as its weakest team. I knew about you, Tom, long before you and Emmy moved out here, and I liked what I knew. You remember how we welcomed you, Milly and I . . ."

I did, I remembered. Milly arrived ten minutes after the moving van. She took my squalling baby out of my arms and off my hands. She brought him back at six o'clock, him and a veal and noodle casserole.

"We were proud to have a couple of your caliber living at the foot of our lane. We were pleased at how you adapted and fit into the community . . ."

Within two weeks Milly had me wearing slacks and collecting for the Red Cross.

"We were pleased to see how you improved the old place, building that beautiful flagstone terrace, Tom, and the outdoor grill. Emmy doing wonders inside here. Milly has never stopped raving about your charming guest room . . ."

A sigh escaped me, a grunt Tom. Bob went on, his voice throbbing, his face growing redder. He was inspired, dedicated to his mission of saving Tom. His gray flannel suit seemed ecclesiastical.

"Tom, boy, it was a thrill to see you making it, and making it you certainly were. Being able to afford to join the country club, buying the Fiat as a station car, getting rid of that motorcycle . . ."

"Say," Tom said, "we won't be needing a second car anymore. How about you buying the Fiat? I'll throw in the lawn mower."

"Riding lessons for Gordy, golf lessons for Emmy. Going to the Vineyard or Nantucket for four or five weeks vacation, instead of two weeks at Asbury Park or Atlantic City like most people . . ."

The golf lessons never did anything for me, really, but, oh, those summers on the islands . . .

"Tom, boy, you have all this, this beautiful life, this beautiful place, because of Madison Avenue. Don't turn your back on the Avenue, boy. The Avenue needs you, you need the Avenue." Bob glanced at his watch. "I've got to go now, but I go knowing I'll see you on that train tomorrow morning with the rest of us." Quickly, Bob said, "Don't speak, boy, think, think! Tom, I shouldn't tell you this just yet, but Jack Carlin is retiring. And you, boy, you are the hands-down favorite to take his place! How do you like that?"

"Who," I asked tremulously, "is Jack Carlin?"

"The fourth in our morning bridge game on the train," Bob said. He went to Tom, clapped him on both shoulders. "For a while Fritz Morgan held out for an older, more experienced man, but I swung him around. We need young blood. So long, fella, you're okay now, I'm sure. We all have our moments when we wish we were in another niche. What you don't realize is that you already are a writer, one helluva writer. There hasn't been as brilliantly sustained writing in America in the past twenty years as your Frozyumyum copy."

Tom sank slowly down, put his head in his hands.

"That's it," Bob said, "think, boy, think."

He winked at me, gave the okay sign, and was gone.

I sat on the sofa beside Tom. "Darling," I said, trying not to sound too plaintive, "I don't really care about Martha's Vineyard and all those beautiful things, but could you get your job back? I mean, could you, for example?"

Tom dropped his hands from his face. A smile began to spread over it and clear up to the roots of his hair.

"Get my job back? No. Not a chance. Never in a million years. Did I ever quit that job!"

"Oh," I said.

"He said that if that's what I thought of the advertising business, he would personally see to it that I would never work on Madison Avenue again."

"Oh," I said. "But Lexington maybe?"

"To Lindstrom, Madison Avenue is a global expression."

"Oh," I said.

"Hi, Gordy," Tom said. "What's wrong?"

"It isn't true, is it?"

"What?"

"Mr. Talbot said you were going back to work tomorrow."

"Mr. Talbot is wrong," Bob said.

"He is?" Gordy was delighted. "You're not?"

"He is. I'm not."

"Boy," Gordy said, "we don't know how lucky we are. Huh, Mom?"

"Go watch television," I said, "and do your homework."

Chapter Six

Breakfasts can be too leisurely. I realized that the next morning when Tom said to Gordy, very man to man, "You don't have to go to college."

"I don't?" Gordy said, pleased.

"He doesn't?" I said, surprised.

"I won't make you," Tom said. "It's up to you."

"What about high school?" Gordy asked.

"Up to you. I want you to lead your own life, make your own decisions. And I'm sure your mother feels the same way."

"Certainly," I said. "Eat your cereal, Gordy."

"Okay. What about the sixth grade next year?"

"Well," Tom said, exhibiting enough moral responsibility to sound a little trapped. "What would you do instead?"

"I'll think of something. I have till next September to make my own decision."

"I'm not sure you get the idea," Tom said. "I don't want you to go through life doing things just because your mother and I want you to do them. Or anybody else. I want you to do things because you want to do them, because you think they're right. Right for you. Understand?"

"Sort of," Gordy said.

"I want you to realize that you should go to school next year and want to go. Because it's right for you to go."

"What about high school?"

"The same."

"College?"

"The same, I hope."

Gordy said sadly, "We're right back where we started. I bet I end up in high school *and* college."

Tom laughed. "Maybe it's a little soon for this discussion. We'll take it up again when you're fourteen or fifteen."

"I'll remind you."

"Boys," Mother said. "The bus."

"I thought maybe Daddy would take me again."

"Sorry, Gordy, but I've got to start writing a novel."

"Are you really going to start today?" I asked. "So soon? I thought you'd take a few days to get organized. Start Monday. Monday's the starting day."

"No, sir! One more cup of coffee and then . . . on second thought, I won't even have another cup of coffee!"

"Attaboy, Pop, give them hell up in the guest room!"

"Let's call it my office, shall we? Em, if anyone calls . . ."

"You're not to be disturbed."

"Under any conditions."

I didn't see Tom again for ten minutes.

"What are you doing, Em?"

"Taking the garbage out."

"I'll do it."

"No, you get back to work."

"Give it to me, for heaven's sake!"

"Well . . . thanks."

"What are you up to now, Em?"

"A washing." I dumped the sheets and pillow cases into the wire laundry basket and picked it up. "Having trouble getting started?"

"Here, let me carry that for you."

"Tom, I've been carrying it for years."

"I can spare a second."

"Ironing?" Tom asked.

"Yes."

"Have much to do?"

"Not so much. How's it going?"

"I just wanted a glass of water." He slowly drank a glass of water. "Well, back to the old desk." He walked slowly to the door. "Got to keep the old nose to the old grindstone. Do you mind ironing?"

"No."

"Therapeutic, huh? It's therapy."

"Yes," I said.

"You know the most? Therapy? Cleaning really dirty wallpaper. When I was a kid I used to visit an aunt in Pittsburgh. Wallpaper got really filthy there. You take this beautiful pink ball of new wallpaper cleaner. I can still smell it, wonderful! And then that first stroke! Cutting through that grime! You feel saintly, you're purifying the world! But I hated cleaning only half-dirty wallpaper. Very unsatisfactory. I guess it's the same difference as converting an agnostic rather than an atheist."

Tom laughed.

I started another handkerchief.

Tom laughed. "Once my aunt walked in when I had just finished writing a dirty word on the dirty wall with the cleaner. Fortunately, I misspelled the word. Aunt Ellen thought I was in the middle of writing Fort Pitt. Well . . ."

"Um-hum," I said.

"Was it Sinclair Lewis who said that the art of writing was applying the seat of your pants to the seat of your chair?"

"Yes," I said.

"How right he was!" Tom slammed a fist into the palm of his other hand. "To work!"

He strode out of the kitchen. He got as far as the hall. I heard the front door open and close. In a few minutes he came into the kitchen from the back yard.

"You know," he said, "I've just been looking at our privet hedge."

"Really?"

"Yeah!"

"So?"

"It looks damn good."

"Tom! Darling! Why don't you relax? You're not set to start writing yet. Start Monday. Take the weekend off, for heaven's sake!"

"Okay."

Milly Talbot telephoned just after dinner.

"Emmy," she said, "Bob's sick."

"Oh, I'm sorry. Is he in bed?"

"No, no, he's sick about Tom. Literally sick. So am I."

"Milly, let's not all get sick yet. This might work out, it just might. Let's give Tom a chance."

"When Tom wasn't on the train this morning, Bob couldn't believe it. But he says not to give up, don't lose heart, Emmy. Bob's going to think about how to lick it all weekend."

"Aren't you going to Long Island this weekend?"

"Yes. Bob's sick about Tom, Emmy, literally sick."

"When are you leaving?"

"In a few minutes. Literally sick."

"Have a good time, Milly."

"Thank you . . . coming, Bob! 'Bye, Emmy."

" 'Bye."

Back in the living room Tom said, "Who was that?"

"Red Cross," I said.

On Saturday morning Tom got up early. On Sunday he got up early. He was keeping in shape for Monday. He was really getting set.

He would have his breakfast, read the paper for a maximum of twenty minutes. Then he'd take a brisk walk, come home, march upstairs, and be at his desk on the dot of eight. He was back downstairs each morning at a minute after eight, glowing with pride at the success of his run-through.

He bought a journal to start as of Monday, but he didn't wait till then to make his first entry. On Saturday afternoon, with Gordy and me in the audience, he wrote, "Monday . . . at my desk at eight. Began novel." Gordy and I applauded. He did an encore. "Tuesday . . . at my desk at eight. Rewrote beginning, finished first chapter." Gordy said "Wow!" Tom took him bowling.

Sunday afternoon Tom said, "We'll have two cocktails, no more. Then an early dinner . . . something light. Lamb chops?"

"I've got some in the freezer."

"Good. Then maybe read a little, watch some television . . . 'What's My Line?' and the news, to see what kind of a day it's been, and then to bed by eleven-thirty. Right?"

"Right," I said.

"Right," Gordy said. " 'At my desk at eight. Began novel.' "

"Right," Tom said.

"Wow!" Gordy said, to see if Tom would take him bowling again. But he didn't. He was too excited for anything as sedentary as bowling.

We had our two cocktails. Gordy, entering into the spirit of the thing, had two cokes. The toasts to tomorrow morning at eight were numerous.

"I'll put on the chops," I said.

"Wait," Tom said, "one more. After all."

All three of us had one more. Then Tom, to his dismay, discovered he had made too much martini. "Waste not," he said, pouring our fourth, "want not."

Gordy groaned. "Do I have to have another coke?"

"It's the eve," Tom said sternly, "of a big day."

"I," Gordy said, "have to be at *my* desk at eight-*thirty!*"

"How about a glass of milk?" Tom suggested.

"Or a lamb chop?" Gordy asked wistfully.

"I'll put them on," I said.

"Good idea," Tom said. "Put on Gordy's lamb chops."

I put them all on. While I was getting dinner on the table, Tom didn't just stand around. He carefully selected a wine from our cellar of three half-empty bottles. Finally, after extensive tasting, he chose what he called a quiet wine but not without a voice of its own. The wine and Tom kept talking to each other all through dinner.

When I came downstairs at ten from seeing Gordy off to sleep, Tom had carefully selected our one bottle of brandy. He was now so excited about tomorrow he couldn't sit still. He kept walking back and forth between his chair and the bottle of brandy.

Having been a writer's wife for only three or four days, I didn't know what to do. A writer's enthusiasm is certainly a very delicate thing. A wife's carping, no matter how logical, quite possibly could dampen it more completely than too much brandy. I decided to try sulking in a corner with a book. Tom didn't seem to notice my disapproval.

"I don't know," he murmured monumentally.

I refused to be intrigued.

"I really don't know," he said, making his ignorance even more monumental, but I was steadfast and kept on reading. "It's important," he said, "damn important." And to prove it he poured himself another monumental drink. "Let's not minimize it. It could be the difference between success and failure."

I turned a page.

"Please, Em."

I put down my book. "All right. The difference between success and failure."

"Thomas Wade," Thomas Wade intoned. "Thomas Wade."

He looked at me, waiting. "Yes?" I said.

"How does it sound to you?"

"Thomas Wade?" I asked. "Thomas Wade?"

Thomas Wade nodded gravely.

"Okay."

He pursed his lips thoughtfully, poured himself another brandy. "Tom Wade," Tom Wade said bluntly. "Tom Wade. Would you be more likely to buy a book by Thomas Wade or Tom Wade?"

"Oh," I said.

"Or Thomas S. Wade. Or Thomas Samuel Wade?"

"How about T. S. Wade?"

"T. S. Wade," T. S. Wade said, enunciating with precision, testing. "T. S. Wade . . . oh, I get it. Come on, Em, this is serious!"

"Too serious to decide tonight. We should sleep on it. Let's go right upstairs and start sleeping on it."

"Sleep?" Tom asked incredulously. "Sleep?"

"This is important enough to justify a pill. I'll take one, too."

"T. Samuel Wade," T. Samuel Wade retorted, reaching for the bottle of brandy. "T. Samuel . . ."

The next morning Gordy asked, "Where's Daddy?"

"Still sleeping," I said.

That afternoon when Gordy came home from school at quarter of three, he asked, "Where's Daddy?"

"Still sleeping," I said.

Chapter Seven

Two hours later, when Gordy and I got home from the dentist, the shades in our bedroom windows were up. We went in the back door. Tom's breakfast setting had been cleared away, the kitchen was immaculate and the dishwasher was humming. As we crossed the dining room I could hear the washing machine at work beneath us. In the living room I could hear the electric waxer churning.

We found Tom waxing the television-room floor.

"Hi," he said, snapping off the machine.

"Hi," Gordy and I said.

"Overslept," Tom said.

"But you're certainly making up for it," I admitted. "The house is throbbing."

"Hated to waste the whole day."

"I did this floor just last week."

"Certainly eats up wax, doesn't it?"

"The dishwasher wasn't full."

"I put in your grandmother's cut glass from the bottom of the dry sink."

"I forgot we had that."

"Filthy," Tom said.

"What have you got in the washing machine?"

"I found a pile of clothes in the hall upstairs."

"They aren't washable."

"Oh."

"No, not washable at all."

"Hi, Gordy," Tom said. "Have a good day at school?"

"Okay. You'll have to erase, won't you, Daddy?"

"What?"

" 'At desk at eight. Started novel.' "

Tom laughed, but not wholeheartedly. "Right, Gordy. I've learned my lesson. That brandy." He ruffed Gordy's crew cut. "Stay off the brandy, kid."

Tuesday the typewriter started clicking before I started making the beds. It went on all morning in the most heavenly little spurts. A few minutes' pause, then clickety-clickety-click. I could imagine him . . . scowling, rubbing the back of his neck, lighting cigarettes, perhaps doing a little traditional pacing, then inspiration and the words flowing onto the paper. He worked like that all morning, steadily.

"Em, has the mail come?"

"It's much too early."

"Good, I want to get this stuff in the box."

"Heavens, what a stack! What have you been doing?"

"Paid all our bills."

"I thought you were working! You were writing checks . . . typing the envelopes."

"Em, I couldn't get started with all these odds and ends cluttering my desk."

"They weren't cluttering yours, they were cluttering mine. You rifled my desk."

"All right, the point is that now I'm really set for tomorrow. Really set."

Wednesday the sound was different, a much more steady pounding of the keys, and in stretches much too long to be addressing envelopes. It was lovely to listen to, like pennies from heaven falling into a bank, your bank. It lasted till lunch.

I refrained from asking any wife-type questions about his day at the office, but when he was out shooting baskets with Gordy I couldn't resist it. You can only go so long not knowing whether your husband writes like James Gould Cozzens or Max Shulman. I crept upstairs to his office. Just one little peek.

The first thing I saw was the waste basket, foaming with yellow balls of paper. Then I saw the single yellow sheet beside the typewriter and the one in it. He was obviously a perfectionist. What mind-wringing labor must have gone into that page and a half! Then, too, his heaped ash tray told the strain, the struggle he had gone through. No wonder it had been such agony for him to get started. But he had, now he had. I felt myself trembling, as playwrights' wives must tremble on opening nights on Broadway. The curtain was going up on my husband's career. I almost didn't dare look. I had to force myself down into the swivel chair. I took a deep breath and began to read.

"Dear Windy,
    Frankly, I don't know how to begin this letter, old pal."

Depleted, I fell back into the swivel chair. Its groan was mine. Tom had spent his morning writing a letter. I saw the waste basket beneath me, the ash tray. He certainly hadn't known how to begin it. My eyes focused again.

"It's been over fifteen years since we used to lie awake nights in our crumby room at the Tau Kappa house and spin our dreams to each other. Yours were political, you in government, the Senate, the Cabinet, someday the Supreme Court. I wanted to be a writer, remember? Well, kid, I finally made it. I am a writer.

"I don't know how to say this, Windy, without making it sound gloating. I'm sure you got a bad deal on being involved in that graft case and some day soon you'll be cleared, out of jail (to put it bluntly) and once more hold public office. Keep our dreams going, kid.

"But about me. I quit my job, resigned from the rat

race and at last I am my own boy and a writer. It's going to be a novel. It won't be easy, I know that, but fortunately I married a girl . . . well, Windy, she's only the greatest in the world. (Who the hell did you marry?) It's unbelievable how understanding and sympathetic Emmy is. She's always in there with the encouraging word and the slap on the back when I need it most. In a word, she's inspiring. I couldn't do this without her.

"And furthermore. You can have Gina, Sophia and Mamie Van Doren all rolled up in one. I'll take Emmy. Know what I mean? But maybe it's thoughtless of me to go on in this vein with you having been (to put it bluntly) in jail for so long . . ."

The next morning Tom realized, just in the nick of time, what was wrong. He had been rushing to his desk before he was completely awake and ready. In his overpowering, headlong desire to get writing, he had been neglecting to take his brisk walk. I watched him stride away, his legs pumping, his arms swinging, head high, breathing deeply. This was walking at its briskest.

He was back in five minutes.

"Damn," he said, limping, "twisted my ankle."

"Oh, Tom! Want a doctor?"

"No. Em, this is Thursday . . ."

"Yes," I said, remembering from the letter to Windy how understanding I was, "why don't you take the rest of the week off and really get lined up for Monday?"

"Really get lined up for Monday."

"Yes, really. Now, relax, enjoy the weekend."

"Maybe I'll play some golf."

On Saturday night Tom didn't have anything to drink before dinner except beer. And nothing with dinner except beer. To make sure that he would keep on with nothing except beer, right after dinner he went to a neighbor's and borrowed half a case of beer.

"It might," he said mysteriously but significantly as I came down from Gordy. "It just might."

I picked up my book and went into my corner.

"You know what? It just very well might."

I buried my nose in the book so deeply that the print blurred.

"Wait," Tom said, "I'll be right back." He went into the kitchen and opened another can of beer. Then, good as his word, he was right back. He held the can up to the light, drank it slowly. "Beer," he said, "the workingman's drink. Where were we? Oh, yeah . . . yep. It . . . just . . . very . . . well . . ."

I gave up and together we said, "Might."

"Make a play," Tom said.

"Oh," I said. "A play."

"One thing, though . . . I'd never let Kazan touch it, direct it. Or Meredith. Logan, maybe. Maybe Josh."

"Josh who?"

"Logan," Tom said impatiently.

"Oh, I didn't realize you were still considering him."

"I wonder if I should adapt it myself."

"Won't you be too busy with your second book?"

"Mandel did a beautiful job on the Drury book."

"So maybe him, huh?"

"But not Gibson, never in a million years. Or Vidal."

"Gore?"

"Or Lawrence," Tom said flatly, "and Lee."

"Or Lindsay," I said, equally unequivocally, "and Crouse."

"I don't know about Crouse," Tom said.

"Ask Lindsay." I rose. "Good night, dear."

"Or Chayefsky."

"Paddy?" I started for the door.

"Good night."

"Or Dore."

"Hunky? Good night, dear."

That night I had the first of my dreams.

"Mrs. McGraw," Jack said, "where are you from?"

"Kingsville, Kansas."

"And how," Jack said, "are things in Kingsville?"

"Awful."

"Glad to hear it," Jack said. "And how are things with you?"

"Miserable."

"Great!" Jack said giggling. "Let's hear about it. No cheers, please, from the audience."

"I'm out of work and my husband left me with seven children by a former marriage of his without a cent or anything edible in the house. Then the house burned down and we moved into a tent until the tornado . . ."

The Misery Meter hit the halfway mark.

"And now," Jack said, "our second contestant!"

"I have this broken neck and the brace keeps rubbing and it makes me irritable so that I yell at the kids and they get sore and hide my crutches so I can't go to my job, a waitress, ten hours a day, and the boss is always making a pass at me . . ."

The Misery Meter hit the three-quarter mark.

"And now our third contestant!"

"My husband is home all day," I said. "He wants to be a writer . . ."

The Misery Meter hit the top.

"Mrs. Wade!" Jack shrieked. "Queen for a Day!"

Chapter Eight

With nothing to do, I wandered around the living room, looking at our books. I was pulling down a collection of Dorothy Parker when I saw *Little Women*. I took it down instead to see if the glove scene could still make me cry. It could, and I was delighted to find that I hadn't become callous in the past two years.

Through my tears I saw Gordy come across the lawn with a new friend of his I don't especially admire. A certain Leonard Bradshaw. There's something too knowing about that Leonard. For instance, I get the impression that he knows we grownups don't know what the hell we're doing. This makes him a little patronizing, which I find unbecoming in an eleven-year-old.

The kitchen door banged. Gordy's books banged down on the sink. He said, "Hi, Dad, where's Mom?"

"In the living room, I think."

"Hi, Mom!"

"Hi," I sobbed.

"Gordy," Tom said, "introduce me to your friend."

"Oh, sorry. Leonard, this is Mr. Wade. Mr. Wade, Leonard."

"I'm his father, Leonard."

"I can see that," Leonard said. "There's a strong family resemblance around your noses. What are you doing, Mr. Wade?"

"Defrosting the refrigerator," Tom said.

Disillusioned with beer as a workingman's drink, and off the hard stuff, Tom gave sherry its chance. Very small glasses of sherry, one at a time.

"I wonder," he said. "You know, I wonder."

I closed my book.

"Anyway, she's a possibility."

I put down my book.

"Lauren Bacall," Tom said, pouring.

"Oh, of course," I said. "The movie of it."

"Maybe Doris Day."

"Doris Day? Why, she's as different from Lauren Bacall as night from . . . oh, sorry."

"You know, Jayne Mansfield is a better actress than people give her credit for."

I rose; sherry, too, had let Tom down.

"Ingrid Bergman . . ."

"Good night, dear."

"Betty Hutton . . ."

"Good night."

"Where's Daddy?" Gordy asked.

"Still sleeping," I said. "Here comes the bus."

"No, sir," Tom said, "you keep your cleaning woman. Look at it this way. I'm saving fifty-two dollars a month on commutation, three or four dollars a day on lunches, a lot on not having haircuts so often, shoeshines, an evening paper . . . for God's sake, you could have Mrs. Sill another day a week!"

DEPOT LIQUOR STORE

"Let us keep you in good spirits."

6 Depot Street   CA 7-0606

March $142.80

COMMUNITY CLEANERS
"In By Ten. . . . . . . .Out By Five"
Lawler Square   CA 7-1141

March $1.65

"Tom, boy," Bob Talbot said, "it's later than you think."

"The twentieth, isn't it?"

"I didn't mean that, damn it . . ."

"It is the twentieth, though, isn't it?"

Bob glanced at his watch. "Nineteenth. Listen to me, Tom . . ."

"Sure you're not slow?"

"Nineteenth. Tom, you . . ."

"Maybe you forgot to wind it."

"Self-winding. Tom . . ."

"I knew a fellow had more trouble with a watch like that. It lost a month every two weeks."

"Tom, there isn't an abler man in the field than my psychiatrist. He knows Madison Avenue and Madison Avenue knows him. Emmy, he'd have Tom back on the Avenue in no time . . ."

"It's a tough decision," Tom said, pouring what was probably mead. "A tough decision."

"Yes, dear?"

"Maybe the Book-of-the-Month Club."

"Oh."

"Or possibly the Literary Guild."

"Good night, dear."

"Or even the Book Find Club."

"Yours would certainly be a challenge for them. Good night, dear."

"Still sleeping," I told Gordy. "Here comes the bus."

Dear Mother,
   You know you're always welcome and we'd love to see you, but just at the moment, things are a little unsettled here. For one thing, the guest room . . .

Dear Windy,
   Great to hear from you. Sure we've got stacks of paper back books around here and I'd be only too glad to send them to you and the boys there. Glad to see you haven't lost your sense of humor, kid. I mean that crack of yours about Emmy baking the cake and file.
   Well, Windy, I'm still plugging away. It's a lot tougher than I figured, but I'm not discouraged. Far from it. I haven't actually got anything on paper yet, but I'm thinking and planning all the time, day and night. I find that I think best when I keep active, so I've been helping Emmy with this and that around the house. Very therapeutic, too . . ."

"Mr. Wade," Leonard Bradshaw said incredulously, "what are you doing now?"
   "A little ironing," Tom said, humming.
   "Yes, but what's that you're ironing?"
   "A slip," Tom said, humming.

"Could be," Tom said, pouring. "He did a wonderful book jacket for . . ."
   "Good night, dear."

"Yes, still," I told Gordy. "The bus."

"Emmy," Milly Talbot said, "I see Tom at the supermarket, but never you."

"Sweetheart," Tom said, "I'll find my way out of this. Lots of writers have periods when they . . ."

"Tom! Look what you're doing!"

"What?"

"You've pasted all the green stamps in the blue stamp book."

"I'll put the kettle on. Emmy, don't worry about me. Lots of writers . . ."

"You can't be too careful," Tom said, pouring.

"Yes, dear?"

"About translators. You can lose a lot in translation if . . ."

"Good night," I said.

"Yes, Gordy," I said. "The bus."

"Hey, Pop, shoot some baskets with me . . . hey, Pop!"

"What? Sorry, I was thinking."

"Shoot some baskets with me, huh?"

"Okay. Soon as I finish shelling these peas."

"Sorry, Mrs. Wade," Mrs. Sill said, "you've always been fair to me and I've enjoyed working for you, but I quit."

"Oh, now, Mrs. Sill . . ."

"Sorry, but there just isn't enough work here for the three of us."

"It's happened before," Tom said, pouring.

"Yes, dear?"

"A first novel winning a Pulitzer prize . . ."

"Good night, dear."

"Yes, Gordy," I said.

Chapter Nine

The call came from the principal's office not long after lunch. Mr. Salter's secretary said I was to come to school for a conference. Gordy had got himself into trouble. She didn't know what it was all about, but Gordy was now in Mr. Salter's office and Mr. Salter would appreciate it if I would come at once.

Tom was in Stamford at the premium store near Bloomingdale's, trading in our blue stamps for an electric waffle iron. I quickly got ready for school. It wasn't until I was in the car I had time to really worry.

This had never happened before. Gordy wasn't an "A" student in deportment, but he averaged a firm "B." His occasional offenses were too minor to rate the attention of the principal, a busy and harassed man with Milly and Bob Talbot on his PTA. Obviously it was something more than just being naughty; inattention, whispering, passing notes. Did kids still shoot paper wads in the rocket age? It had to be something serious. Lying, cheating on a test, stealing. Oh, dear, I thought.

I found myself checking Gordy's heritage for bad blood that might be cropping out in him. I had an uncle who was considered no good in East Liverpool, Ohio, but in New York or Fairfield County his misbehavior, bottles, and babes would have been looked on simply as something he could afford. At any rate, Gordy couldn't join Uncle Earl's league; he thought liquor smelled funny and babes looked funny. Tom's grandfather on his mother's side disappeared once, the story went, for three days and came home with his hair parted in the middle, but Tom's grandmother immediately forgave him and liked his hair the new way. There was nothing on either side of our family slates that could reflect unfavorably on Gordy. Quite the contrary.

Certainly Gordy was incapable of any serious wrongdoing. Certainly no one could be a better judge of that than a boy's own mother. Gordy was being held unfairly in the principal's office. I stepped harder on the gas.

By the time I got to the school I was in such a state of motherly indignation that I shall be ashamed forever. I made a spectacle of myself. I stomped into the ranch-type school, down the corridor hung with the kids' ranch-type art work and into Mr. Salter's outer office. His secretary rose from her desk, alarmed.

"Mrs. Wade?"

"Exactly!"

I stomped past her, flung open the door of the inner office. Mr. Salter rose from behind his desk, alarmed. Gordy jumped up from his chair in the corner.

"Mom!" he yelped. "What . . ."

"Mrs. Wade," Mr. Salter said, "what . . ."

"Mom, is something wrong at home?"

"At home?" I leveled a finger at Mr. Salter. "Just you listen to me . . ."

"Mom! Mr. Salter didn't do anything! I did!"

"He's made you confess!"

"What? Mom, please sit down or something . . ."

Gordy led me to a chair, seated me, patted me anxiously on the shoulder. His face, flushed with embarrassment, brought me to my senses.

"I'm sorry," I said. "I'm afraid I was upset. Forgive me, Mr. Salter. I'm all right now. How is Mrs. Salter?"

"Couldn't be better, thank you, Mrs. Wade."

"Gordy . . ." I turned back to Mr. Salter. "May Gordy go and see if I turned the ignition off in the car?"

"Of course. Go ahead, Gordy, then wait with Miss Smalley for a moment."

"Yes, sir."

Gordy went off on his errand gratefully. He didn't meet my eyes as he walked past me. He closed the door quietly after him. I couldn't remember him ever having done that before.

Mr. Salter came from behind his desk and sat in Gordy's chair. He didn't seem to be a principal doing his routine duty. He was more a friend of the family, reluctant to tell some bad news.

"Mrs. Wade," he said, "do you know Charley Baker?"

"I think I've heard Gordy mention him."

"Yes. He's in Gordy's class. Charley's a large boy, tall and stout. A voracious feeder, eats constantly, in class and out. We have decided to ignore it, hoping that some day soon Charley will be full. Our only stipulation has been that his peanuts be already shelled and he keep his diet reasonably balanced. There's something not quite satisfactory in that boy's home life. Besides being a compulsive eater, he's a bully. In my time I have seen many, many bullies. Charley outdoes them all. For his bulk he is surprisingly quick on his feet. Not even any of the sixth-grade boys dare tangle with Charley. But this afternoon Gordy did."

"Oh, dear, did he hurt Gordy? I couldn't see any signs of . . ."

"Mrs. Wade, despite the fact that he outweighs Gordy by forty or fifty pounds, Gordy beat the daylights out of him. Reduced him to tears, in fact."

"Well! Gordy!"

"Yes," Mr. Salter said dryly, "if your son exercises his championship, we have a new school bully. Now, although none of us here was exactly dismayed to see Charley get a good thumping at long last, I hope you aren't getting the impression that I've asked you here to congratulate you."

"No, no! But little Gordy . . . sorry. What was the fight about? Was Gordy sticking up for somebody? Defending someone? A girl? A poor little girl?"

Mr. Salter frowned. "There's a problem here, Mrs. Wade, which I don't feel we'll solve if you insist upon regarding Gordy as a combination of Sir Galahad, David, and Sugar Ray Robinson."

"But was this completely Gordy's fault?" I demanded, losing my poise again. "I mean, shouldn't Charley and his mother be here? I mean, we should be fair and hear Charley's side of this, too, the big . . . sorry. What I really mean is, despite Charley's bad record and his eating like a pig, maybe it was partly Gordy's fault, not all Charley's. Maybe Gordy called him "Fatso." He shouldn't have done that. He should be taught that sometimes we must sacrifice accuracy to courtesy. Yes! I will certainly send Gordy to bed without any supper, although it seems to me that if that happened to Charley occasionally the world would be a safer place to live in. Well?"

Mr. Salter was smiling, but also shaking his head. "Hell hath no fury like a mother . . ." Mr. Salter sighed and added, "in my office."

"Oh," I said. "Yes, I see. Sorry."

"Mrs. Wade, this isn't a simple question of discipline. Charley taunted Gordy about something . . ."

"Then Charley did start it! Oh."

"Sorry?"

"Very."

"Yes, Charley did start it by saying something that cut so deeply, that enraged him so he attacked and ferociously whipped a boy twice his size. He won't tell me what it was that disturbed him so. I got the feeling he's ashamed of it. He begged me not to ask Charley what he said. He vowed further vengeance on Charley if he ever repeats it . . . ah, Mrs. Wade, you know what it might be, don't you?"

"Yes," I said.

"Is it so very serious?"

"Oh, dear."

"If there's any way I can help . . ."

"No."

"You can handle it, and you will."

"I hope so. Thank you, Mr. Salter."

Gordy stood up as I closed the door of the principal's office behind me. I said, "Let's go, Gordy."

"Am I allowed?"

"Yes, you're allowed."

"Are you in a hurry?"

"A hurry?"

"I want to get my gym shoes and stuff out of my locker."

"Why?"

"I'm never coming back."

"Oh, Gordy!"

"I'm not, I can't! All the kids . . . I can't ever come back!"

"We'll talk about this at home, shall we?"

"I don't want to go home, either."

"Gordy, you don't sound like a boy big enough to have licked Charley Baker."

"I don't think that was so great."

"Now, there you did sound like a big boy. Beating somebody up isn't so great. You made me remember that. Let's take a ride and talk things over."

"It won't do any good."

I drove under the Connecticut Turnpike and out to the beach. Except for a couple of kite flyers and one of their little sisters and a dog, it was deserted. If only I were bringing Gordy down here to fly a kite. He flies a nice kite. I parked and we sat looking out over the Sound in the direction of Long Island.

"Gordy," I said.

"Let's get out," he said quickly, "and take a walk on the beach."

"I can't. High heels."

He put his hand on the door. "I need the exercise."

"Haven't you had enough exercise for one day?"

"I'm not going back to that school, I'm not."

"Gordy, why did you fight Charley? What did he say?"

"Mom!"

"Yes?"

"Does Daddy know you've come to school?"

"No, he wasn't home."

All mankind's burden seemed to fall from Gordy's shoulders. He swung around to me. "Don't tell him about it! Please don't, promise!"

"Charley said something about your father, didn't he?"

Gordy nodded.

"Something pretty bad."

"You know what it was. You can guess."

"Well, I don't want to make a wrong guess . . ."

"Mom!"

"Gordy?"

"Daddy's just having trouble getting started, isn't he? It's hard to write a book. Especially if you never wrote one before, it's hard, isn't it?"

"Very hard."

"He has to think a lot, all the time. He has to think and he doesn't want to just sit around and think like some dope, so he helps you while he's thinking."

"Yes."

"Yes. He told me. But, gee," Gordy said plaintively, "does he have to help you so much?"

"Well, when a man does as much thinking as your father, he's bound to get quite a lot of housework done. That's what the fight was about?"

"Charley was yelling around that Daddy wears the skirts in

our family. He does the washing and the ironing and every-thing. He wears an apron instead of pants. He kept yelling, 'Hey, Gordy, can he bake a cake?' And I hit him to shut him up and I'll hit him again if he . . . Mom, promise you won't tell Daddy about this! He'd just die if he knew. He's having trouble getting started, he's thinking . . . You've got to promise you won't tell him!"

"I promise, Gordy. I understand."

Gordy sank back in his seat. He was tired. "But what can we tell him when I don't go back to school on Monday?"

"You'll go back to school, Gordy. There's all the weekend. By Monday the kids will have forgotten all about this."

"No. But maybe Daddy will start his book on Monday. Mightn't he? Mightn't he, Mom?"

"Yes," I said. "He just might."

"No," Gordy said, "I bet he won't. And I bet he isn't really thinking when he's doing the housework."

"Gordy, can you see inside his head?"

"I watched him the other day. He had a washing in the machine. He was defrosting the refrigerator and hard-boiling some eggs and singing, 'Working on the railroad all the live-long day.' That doesn't leave much room for thought. Does it, Mom?"

"No," I admitted.

That night I dreamed Ed Murrow came to call.

Chapter Ten

Mona Cobb always has her cocktail parties on Sunday evening. Boyd, her third husband, insists on this. She's only his second legal mate, which gives him a feeling of failure, a sense of inferiority to Mona. He tries to minimize her numerical advantage over him by insisting a lot. For instance, he insists that Mona never wear dark glasses in the house, never wear slacks anywhere, and that they have a cook. Dark glasses make Mona dizzy, she has one of the most prominent, oddly shaped bottoms this side of Pelham Manor, and she considers kitchens a waste of floor space. Boyd is usually this cagey about his insisting, so their's is a happy marriage and it looks as if Boyd will never catch up to Mona without committing bigamy, which is unlike him.

The theory behind Boyd's insistence that Mona's cocktail parties be on a Sunday night is that the boys will go home early to be bright and fresh for work on Monday morning, and not sit around till all hours drinking his liquor. He considers the parties Mona's, but the liquor his. Boyd's Sunday-night theory has been known to break down. There was one memorable occasion when four or five of the boys formed a car pool and drove directly to the Monday morning eight-ten from the party, leaving their wives to trade recipes for Bloody Marys with Mona. Sitters in our part of the country are often able to retire at the age of fifteen.

Nobody would dream of missing one of Mona's parties. Mainly due to her knack with a guest list, her parties are never dull. If there has been a particularly bitter divorce in the neighborhood, Mona carefully sees to it that the couple meet again for the first time at one of her parties. This creates a certain tension that Mona finds delightful. She has been known to import a guest from as far away as Bucks County in order that a man and his wife have an evening together with the man's or the wife's paramour. Let two men call each other fascists at a town meeting about sewage, one woman vow to scratch another's eyes out for any reason, no matter how trivial, Mona will immediately throw a party and secretly bring these enemies together. Mona's Sunday evenings start out very quietly. Everyone is holding his breath.

Gordy had his supper early that Sunday evening. I got him all fixed in the television room and went upstairs to finish dressing. Tom made the initial loop in tying his tie, lifted a can of beer off the bureau, drank deeply, and finished tying his tie, smacking his lips.

He said, "It's true, you know, it's true."

"Oh, no!" I said.

"Yes, an agent can make or break a writer."

"Tom!"

"What?"

"How much beer have you had?"

"Well, let's see. One, two, three . . . then another before lunch, that's four . . . one with lunch, one after, that's six . . . a couple while I was shooting baskets with Gordy, that's eight . . . he beat me . . . two more while Gordy and I watched 'Face the Nation,' that's ten . . . then this one, eleven . . . eleven! My God!"

"Yes."

"That's a lot of beer, you can't deny that."

"Oh, Tom . . ."

"Eleven." He shook his head in awe. "The figures sure mount up. Like the Christmas Club. You save a dollar a week and before you know it, it's Christmas."

"I'm not sure I want to go to this party with you."

"Em, I promise not to drink at the party."

"That's ridiculous."

"Well, just one. To keep up appearances."

"I really am annoyed!"

"But we are going, aren't we? I've hardly been out of the house all week. What's the point of me having this gabardine suit if I never have a chance to wear it?"

"All right, let's go and get it over with. This is the first time I've ever had to do the driving *to* a party."

"You look beautiful," Tom said, finishing his beer.

We went downstairs.

"Good-by, Mom," Gordy said. "Have fun."

"Good-by and thanks."

"So long, Pop."

Tom steadied himself on the doorknob. "Be a good boy," he said. Seriously.

"Okay. Hey, Daddy . . ."

"What, kid?"

"Tomorrow morning," Gordy said. "It's Monday again. At your desk at eight? Give them hell? Finish chapter one?"

"Gordy," Tom said, "I'm sorry you brought that up."

"Oh. Why?"

"Because," Tom said, "I was going to surprise you."

"Hey!" Gordy yelled. "Mom! Did you hear that?"

"Yes, dear, I heard."

"May I have another coke to celebrate?"

"I suppose so."

"Take it easy on the coke, son," Tom said unsteadily.

"Okay! Wow! Finished chapter one! What'll I wear to school tomorrow, Mom?"

"I'll lay something out when I come home."

"Finished chapter one! Hey, boy!"

Most of Mona's regulars were already there; we about completed that group. We were the people Mona knew she could trust. She knew she could rely on us to be all ears at the party, not interrupt anything embarrassing that was going on and then, during the next week, to thoroughly spread the news of whatever appalling had happened near and far.

The party was still in the stage of watchful waiting, which meant the principals hadn't shown up yet. The Cobbs gave us their routine greeting. Mona always screams at the wife, "Who's that sexy, sexy man you're with?" Then she invariably clutches the husband's arm convulsively to her, somehow making his elbow disappear down the front of her décolleté. Boyd always, after jovially clapping the husband on the shoulders so hard that it shakes him loose from Mona's décolleté, offers the first drink by saying, "How about one for the road?" Or, if Daylight Saving Time is keeping the sun in the sky, he might say, "How about a nightcap?" That's about all he ever says during an evening. After everybody gets his first drink he lets his guests fend for themselves and justs stands around worrying about the ice running out.

We went through the ritual with our host and hostess. Tom got the drink that was going to be his one for the evening; so did I, but it was a double martini. We joined the Talbots.

Milly was looking her strange, exotic best. She never failed to surprise me when she put on a dress and took off those formidable glasses she wears so that she can tell one of her children from the others. She isn't really that blind, but at parties she always waits till people speak before she calls them by name. She was drinking a whiskey sour. She likes them very sweet.

Bob was drinking sauerkraut juice. He brings his own to parties. It's amazing how few people can keep sauerkraut juice in the house. Bob, after every sip of every drink, including sauerkraut juice, always says, "Ah, that's more like it!" I've heard him say, "Ah, that's more like it!" after washing down an aspirin.

Bob murmured something that I didn't catch, but his tone and manner were so sepulchral that he seemed to be inquiring about someone who wasn't at the party because he was busy this evening knocking at death's door.

"What, Bob?" Tom asked anxiously.

"I said, how's the novel coming along?"

"Oh," Tom said. "Thanks."

There was an unusually awkward pause. But Bob, having created it, had the grace to destroy it. He said, "Ah, that's more like it!"

Quickly, we joined the fireplace group, whose heads, like cattle in the rain, were all turned in the same direction, no matter how uncomfortable it was for some of them. They were keeping an eye on the door. Ernie and Lereve Kelley, as usual, were doing their utmost to be the life of the party. She, as usual, was confidently telling an amusing little something and he, as usual, made a funny crack every time she stopped for breath. They're all right when they're not together, but they're inseparable.

"This little old New England . . . Puritan cookbook," she was saying, "you can't believe it! The recipes, my God! I remember one . . . 'Take thou four bushels of potatoes, peel. Take thou two pecks of parsley, cleanse. Take thou one ox . . .'"

"Dice," Ernie said.

" 'Take thou two bushels of turnips, three bushels of maize, one bushel of carrots . . .'"

"Serves four," Ernie said.

Quickly, Tom and I joined the bar group, which was able to watch the door in the bar mirror. Harley Nicholson had the situation well in hand. Harley is our raconteur. He needs no help like Ernie Kelley does. This is very convenient as Harley is a bachelor. He's big in local real estate. He is always the first to sense when a divorce is impending, so he gets the inside track on selling the wrecked homes. The amazing number of these he sells every year is probably what has made him leery of marriage for himself.

"An amusing thing happened at the Red Cross Blood Bank last week," Harley said, chuckling. "Of course, you've all heard about it?"

We all nodded or said yes, we had, and Harley went on.

"Jack Billings had already given his blood. It was in the bottle, you know. Well, Jack got it into that big, fat, bullheaded head of his that he didn't want to give his blood after all. He wanted it back. The nurse thought he was kidding at first. When she saw he wasn't, she told him he couldn't have it back . . . they didn't have the equipment there for a transfusion. Jack said he didn't want a transfusion. He wanted the bottle of blood. To take out, as it were. Home. Would she please wrap it up? It was his blood. The nurse said no, legally it wasn't. He had signed it over and so forth . . . but Jack raised such a fuss that the nurse called the big brass. Robin Simpson, I think it was. Robin couldn't believe her ears. She just stood there with her mouth open, listening to Jack rant and rave. Finally, all she could say was, "Indian giver!" So Jack took home his bottle of blood. Well, Peggy, the little woman, was very upset at what Jack had done. You know how conscientious Peggy is. As soon as Jack was well on his way toward drinking himself into his usual evening stupor, she got the thing away from Jack and hid it. She thought she'd take the blood back. Or at least return the empty bottle. About midnight Jack came to a little and started looking for his blood. He couldn't find it anywhere . . . and Peggy kept saying she hadn't seen it since he brought it home. So about twelve-thirty Jack calls the police and says he would like to report . . ."

"A serious loss of blood," we all said, and joined in Harley's laughter.

"That reminds me," Harley said, "you all remember the story of Mac McGill and the cellar door, of course."

We all nodded or said that we remembered it perfectly.

"Well," Harley said, "Mac McGill was putting in a new

cellar door about three years ago . . . one of those aluminum deals and . . ."

We all turned away from Harley. His voice faded out on a note of awe. Silence seeped through the room, lapped up against the walls. One of Mona's finest hours was surely striking.

The absolute epitome of the Other Woman was slithering into the room. She didn't signify that to only me. Every female mouth present tightened in disapproval, envy, and dread, mostly dread. Mona's import for tonight was easily the most feared woman in all the East. There was no use describing her. A description of her face and figure would merely add up to some run-of-the-mill, everyday pornography. This babe had something plus the physical. She breathed the illicit; the low, pink light of the love nest glowed from her.

Behind her, like a symbol, was a huge man, bursting with vitality. He had steel-gray hair, a crew cut that was not unsuitable for polo, too. His face was florid under a tan as old as he. He looked as though he had just had his picture in *Life*, his biography in *Fortune*, and a full report of his latest hard-hitting message to industry in *Time*.

As we girls trembled, Mona led Other Woman and her escort to our group. I looked around the circle of men, their mouths wide open like greedy, inane birdlings in a nest. Tom wasn't one of them. He was at the bar, pouring himself a large drink. He gulped it down, shuddering under its impact. Never have I seen a human being so obviously need a bigger drink in a bigger hurry. Stunned, I turned to face Other Woman.

"Everybody," Mona said, drooling with anticipation, "this is Sandra Cummings."

Mona introduced each of the group to her individually. I fixed a smile on my face, knowing it would take plastic surgery to get it off. My turn came.

"And this," Mona said, slipping her arm cozily around mine, preventing flight, "is Emmy." Then she added, hitting so far below the belt my shins ached, "Emmy Wade, wonderful mother, wonderful cook, just plain, plain wonderful."

"Wonderful," Sandra said, making it sound more like "plain," though.

She said it throatily, of course. Her voice was a husky murmur, naturally. She clasped my hand warmly in hers. Between the two of them, Sandra and Mona, they had me pinioned. For a moment I thought they were going to throw me in the pool or toss me in a blanket. For not being a good sport. I rallied, got my eyes open again, said, "Glad to meet you."

She said, "I feel as though I know you, Mrs. Wade. Emmy."

"Really?" I said.

"Tom," she said, "has spoken of you so often."

"Really?" I said.

"He certainly adores you," she said. She took a hand of Tom's in that other one of hers. "Hello, Tom. She's everything you said she was, and more."

"Hiya, Sandy," Tom said. "Emmy, Sandy is Mr. Lindstrom's secretary." He turned to the *Time-Life-Fortune* man. "Hiya, Mr. Lindstrom."

Mr. Lindstrom nodded, just barely perceptibly.

"You know each other!" Mona trumpeted in her social scream. "But, of course! I should have realized!" She slyly, but not without some pride, divulged her chicanery to the whole group. "Mr. Lindstrom is the head of Tom's old agency. Well! Isn't this a coincidence? Mr. Lindstrom, however do you get along without Tom?"

"We manage," Mr. Lindstrom said. "The industry has survived."

"But I'm sure," Mona said, "the office can't be the same without Tom."

"We must make sacrifices," Mr. Lindstrom said, "to the Great American Novel."

"Tom," Mona said, "what's it about, your novel?"

"This," Tom said, weaving slightly, "and that. It's definitive."

"About advertising? Madison Avenue? Of course, it is, isn't it? And Mr. Lindstrom will be in it! I'm dying to read it!"

"Wade," Mr. Lindstrom said, "I'm warning you. If there's anybody in your book even slightly resembling me or any of my friends . . ."

"Living or dead," Tom said, "it will be purely coincidental."

"Son," Mr. Lindstrom said, suddenly, alarmingly charming, "come back to the shop where you belong. You talk our language. You've got the genuine touch. You're a born copywriter. How about it, son?"

"Let's put it through the wringer," Tom said, weaving less slightly, "to see how it dries."

"Novelists are a dime a dozen . . ."

"Let's soak it overnight," Tom said, "to see if it shrinks."

"Anyone can write a novel . . ."

"Let's put it in the freezer," Tom said, "to see how it thaws."

"You didn't mean all the things you said about advertising . . ."

"Let's tell it to Sweeney," Tom said, "let's send it once around the track . . ."

"My God, you couldn't have meant all those things!"

"Let's put it on base . . ."

"The opium of the people! That's communistic talk, Wade!"

"Let's hang it on the Christmas tree . . ."

"You owe me an apology! You owe the whole industry an apology!"

"Let's send it into orbit . . ."

"By God, I want to talk to you, Wade!" Mr. Lindstrom was livid. "Come outside with me!"

He took Tom's arm, pulled him away from the bar.

"Hey!" Tom said. "Let's not yank my arm from its socket to see if it . . ."

Tom jerked away from Mr. Lindstrom, pushed him off.

Mr. Lindstrom said, quite justifiably, I thought, "Why, you drunken b–st–rd, you silly s–n–v–b–tch!"

Tom said, "You H–dd–n P–rsuad–r! You St–tus S—ker! You W–ste M–ker! And, in closing, you P–r–m–d Cl–mb–r!"

There was a shocked buzz from the crowd that grew into angry resentment against Tom. He had gone too far. There are certain words better left unsaid in these parts, and Tom had used all eight of them. The men moved behind Mr. Lindstrom to a man, forming a solid wall of support. They stood silent, grim, an ugly, menacing mob, and Mr. Lindstrom was their champion. Slowly he raised his righteous, livid fists.

"My God!" a woman's voice whispered frantically. "Someone pass the hors d'oeuvres!"

But as Mr. Lindstrom moved inexorably forward, Mona stepped between him and Tom. I looked at my watch. It was just ten to nine. I shouldn't have worried. It was much too early for fighting. Mona never let things get really out of hand, actually violent, that is, until the party was about over anyway. She thoroughly approved of her parties being broken up by fights, but at the proper time and place . . . out in the parking area where everybody would be handy to their cars after the fight. Mona's a stickler for form; there are ways of doing things.

She pressed Tom's arm to her. "Now, now," she said, "come along. You, too, Emmy, darling. There's someone else here I know you'll just love meeting. I invited them especially for you."

"It's the old Reach place," Mona said.

"The *old* Reach place," Fred said.

"Damp days," Lois said, "I can still smell old Reach."

"I'm surprised," Mona said, "you all haven't met before."

"I never get out," Lois said.

"I mean," Mona said, "you both have a son the same age."

"Yes," Tom said, obviously just to be saying something, "we have a son the same age. You do, too, huh?"

"What's that again?" Fred said.

"Thick," Lois said.

"They both," Mona said, her eyes dancing, and I could see it all now, "they both go to school together. Gordon and Charles."

"Gordon," Fred said.

"That's ours," Tom said.

A little exasperated, Mona spelled it out for Fred. "Gordon Wade . . . Gordy Wade!"

"Gordy Wade," Fred said, "the bully!"

"Yes!" Mona said and, having done her bit, she relaxed.

"Gordy Wade," Fred said, "the bully!"

"Charley's bigger than Gordy," I said.

Tom said, "What's all this?"

"As if you didn't know!" Fred said scathingly.

"I don't," Tom said.

"Too busy washing and ironing, eh, to keep an eye on your kid? Too busy with the cooking!" Fred took a swing at Tom, missed. "Too busy at the supermarket!" Fred took another swing at Tom, missed. "Baking and cleaning! Pantywaist!"

Fred crouched, led with his left, tucked his chin behind his shoulder, circled Tom, bobbing and weaving on the balls of his feet. He was a picture fighter if I ever saw one. His left snaked out and jabbed the air in front of Tom's eyes, viciously, then he backed away, dancing. Mona really had herself a very promising boy here; with careful handling he could reach the top of her guest list.

Chapter Eleven

Mona moved Tom and me away from Mr. Lindstrom and his posse to a group huddled, less fearfully now, in the terrace doorway. It gave way before us, backed out on the terrace, became self-consciously very, very social. Behind us the angry, sullen silence was broken by a voice saying, "Ah, that's more like it!" The sauerkraut juice was flowing again.

Mona steered us forcibly to a solid-looking couple with surprisingly long arms and low foreheads. It was as though this had drawn them romantically together; it couldn't have been a coincidence. The man had had a lot to drink and was obviously proud of how well he was holding it. He was rigid. His wife, too, had had lots, but she didn't seem to care one way or another how she held it. She was limp. I couldn't remember ever seeing either of them before. They looked blankly at us.

Mona said brightly, "Fred and Lois Baker . . . Emmy and Tom Wade."

The Bakers and the Wades shook hands. It seemed to take longer than usual. I understood why when I found Tom shaking hands with me. I squeezed his hand as hard as could, but it didn't do any good. He needed a cold shower.

"The Bakers," Mona said, "have only lived here about a year."

"Really?" I said, although I didn't actually doubt it.

"Yes," Fred said, verifying it, "about a year."

"It seems longer," Lois said.

"They have a beautiful house," Mona said.

"A beautiful house," Fred said.

"You're never home," Lois said.

"Pantywaist!" Fred snarled again.

Tom swung his right, missed. He tried his left, missed. They took to circling each other.

"Let him have it, Tom!" Lois said, then she turned to me. "You and Tom must come over sometime soon."

"We'd love to," I said.

"Cute dress."

"The Bandbox."

"The chin, Tom, the chin!" Lois called across the terrace. "He's just like Charley, the chin! The Bandbox . . . where is that?"

"Across from the big bank."

"Oh, yes. You go there, Mona?"

"Sometimes," Mona said, watching Fred and Tom unhappily.

Tom desperately threw a right from way back and stumbled over an end table. Potato chips flew and a glass broke. A few people drifted onto the terrace to see what was happening. They couldn't tell that Fred and Tom were fighting. They went right back into the living room. The boys were pretty much winded now; their circling was barely discernible, their fists hardly raised.

"I don't trust our sitter," Lois said. "She empties the icebox. Lovely time, Mona. See you, Emmy. Come on, Fred. Nice meeting you, Tom."

She led Fred out to the cars.

"Well," Tom said, brushing potato chips off his jacket and smoothing his hair. "I didn't come out of that too badly."

"You should see the other guy," I said. "He's immaculate."

"What was that all about? Cooking, ironing, pantywaist?"

"Let's go home."

"It had something to do with Gordy fighting their boy . . . did you know he did?"

"Yes."

"Why didn't you tell me about it?"

"Tom, you're in no shape to discuss this now."

"Why didn't you tell me?"

"Gordy made me promise not to."

"Why?"

"Tom, please, let's go home."

"Because he was ashamed. Ashamed of me. I need a drink."

"If you have another drink, I'm going home without you. Now."

"Now, Em, we never do that. Just one more drink."

I put the car in the garage, then stood for a moment in the drive. It was a lovely night, stars, moon, all that. I thought I saw the curtains move in Gordy's room. When I got there he was in bed, pretending to be asleep, but the grim expression on his face betrayed him. He had seen that I had come home alone. There must have been something I could have said to him, something comforting, reassuring, but nothing occurred to me. I gently pressed a kiss on his forehead to make him think I thought he was asleep. Never have I felt less adequate.

Foolishly, I went to bed. I couldn't even pretend to sleep. Sensibly, I put on a robe, went downstairs and paced the living room. It looked lovely, pictures, books, all that. The fourth time, at half-hour intervals, I started to dial Mona's number, a car stopped outside. It was the Talbots' station wagon. Milly got out of it and came into the kitchen. She was furious.

"I've got your husband in the back of the station wagon," she said. "I'll help you unload him, if you still want him."

"It's that bad."

"It's incredible, it's been an incredible evening."

"One of Mona's best parties. Where's Bob?"

"That swine," Milly said, thin-lipped.

"Bob a swine?"

"He hasn't been so drunk since the fourth was born. He wanted a boy."

"Bob drunk? But he wasn't drinking anything but . . ."

"Your Tom spiked his sauerkraut juice," Milly said, her lips disappearing completely. "It was disgusting. Besides ruining all that good sauerkraut juice."

"Where is Bob?"

"I stopped at our place. He crawled out of the back and staggered into the house without saying a word to me. Like I was a paid chauffeur. If his stumbling around wakes even one of the girls, I'll skin him. You should thank your lucky stars you came home. They were disgusting. Sitting there with their arms around each other."

"Oh. The old pal bit."

"Bob told Tom how much he admired him, told him over and over again. Said Tom was doing what everybody on Madison Avenue wanted to do, but only Tom has the talent and guts."

"Bob said that?"

"Tom spiked his sauerkraut juice. They're going to collaborate on a novel. Under the name of Wade Talbot and they want Clara Bow to do the movie."

"Oh, Lord, that."

"They're going to begin work at eight sharp tomorrow. Tom insisted they work in your guest room, but Bob insists on using our guest room. I'll see him in hell first."

"Milly, you know Bob'll be on the eight-ten in the morning."

"Yes, but it scares me to think what might be going on in that man's subconscious. In all their subconsciouses. Oh, God, I'm exhausted. I think I'll only send two of the girls to school tomorrow."

"Would you like a drink?"

"No one in our family is ever going to touch another drop. Let's empty the station wagon."

It wasn't until we got the body out onto the drive that I said, "Milly, this is Bob."

"Oh, damn! I never made that mistake before."

"Milly, you really should wear your glasses."

"Oh, God!"

"What?"

"Tom's probably in our bed. No, I doubt if he could get up the stairs. Well, let's put this one back and then get them sorted out right."

"Bob's trying to say something, Milly."

"What, you swine?"

"Hoot Gibson," Bob said.

I dreamed one of my dreams that night.

"First of all," the kindly man said, "I want to thank Capitol Airlines for bringing Mrs. Wade here, and TWA for bringing Mr. Wade here. Mr. Wade is here, isn't he? Oh, not yet. Well, while we're waiting . . . what's that? Oh, sorry. TWA would like me to make it clear that *they* brought Mrs. Wade, and Capitol . . . uh . . . has Mr. Wade. Let me say to our audience that we are in no way trying to exploit Mr. and Mrs. Wade's marital difficulties. By being on television we hope that someone watching our program will profit by Mr. and Mrs. Wade's frank discussion of their problems and by any advice or counseling of mine. The Institute's doors are always open. Oh, Mr. Wade."

"Sorry," Tom said. "What a way to run an airline."

"Quite all right," the doctor said hastily. "Now both of you, Mr. and Mrs. Wade, are attractive, intelligent people. How long have you been married?"

"Eleven years," Tom said.

"Twelve," I said.

"You have your own home?"

"Yes," Tom said.

"It's in his name," I said.

"Do you have any financial worries?"

"No," Tom said.

"Yes," I said.

"Is there an in-law problem?"

"Some," Tom said.

"None," I said.

"How many children do you have?"

"One," Tom said.

"Is that correct, Mrs. Wade?"

"Yes," I said.

"You see," the kindly doctor said, "it is possible to find an area of agreement. Let us proceed from there . . ."

Chapter Twelve

"There go Francine's books," I said.

Gordy grunted.

"I owe you another nickel."

Gordy didn't care; he glanced up the stairs.

"Here come the Talbots," I said doggedly. "Has she got all the girls? One, two, three, four. That answers my question. She's got all the girls."

Gordy wasn't listening to me; he was listening to our bedroom. I kept trying.

"Timmy and Jim aren't hitting each other this morning. What's wrong? Have they had a fight?"

Gordy sneaked another look up the stairs.

"Here comes the bus."

Gordy dropped his books.

"Francine!" I said. "Really!"

"I'm not going to school."

"Oh, now Gordy . . ."

"I'll just have to beat up Charley again."

"They've forgotten by now."

"Seeing me will remind them."

"Pick up your books."

"Mom! I can't go to school! The kids . . ."

"Pick up your books, young man."

"You're mad at me! You ought to be mad at him!"

"I'm mad, Gordy, I'm mad, but please go to school!"

"Okay!" He snatched up his books. "But I'm only going because I don't want to stay around here!"

He slammed out of the house. He ran to the bus, rudely jostled his way through the group at the door. An older boy pushed him back. Gordy hit him on the arm with all his might. Danny jumped out of the driver's seat, scolding. Gordy got on the bus, his head hanging.

I turned away, walked into the living room, wondering why I had insisted Gordy go to school. I hadn't been sympathetic or understanding, put myself in his place. I had been an automatic parent. Go to school, pick up your books, Mother said, and go to school . . .

There were frantic footsteps overhead. Then Tom was on the stairs, struggling to get his bathrobe on over his pajamas as he plunged toward the front door.

"Hey, Gordy!" he shouted.

He jerked open the door and was out of sight. A horrible dread upset my stomach, but my legs walked me out into the hall. I saw Tom pushing toward the bus, his bathrobe flying ludicrously out behind him, only one of his arms in it. He caught up to the last of the Talbot girls. He nudged her and Milly aside. He climbed into the bus. Into the very bus itself. He was on the school bus in his pajamas and half of the bathrobe I had given him for Christmas six years ago.

Milly gaped at him, wobbling her head. No one in her family had ever got on the bus in that condition. Tom started down the aisle, looking for his son. I saw his son sink down in his seat and disappear, perhaps forever.

Tom stopped dead, as though paralyzed. Then a big boy stood up, grinning, and held his bathrobe for him. Tom put his arm in its sleeve and pulled the front together, modestly. The boy, with a large gesture of mock gallantry, offered Tom his seat. The kids shrieked with laughter. A girl in the front of the bus picked up one of Tom's slippers. It was elaborately passed down the aisle to him. He took it and looked at it for what seemed hours. Then a smile of recognition broke across his face. He nodded affectionately and put it on.

The kids cheered. Milly was beckoning wildly to Tom. Danny, rendered immobile with disbelief, was still collapsed on the steering wheel. I died for Gordy. I could imagine him trying desperately to worm his way down through the floor of the bus and into the ground.

Tom seemed to come to. He wiped his hands across his eyes, shook his head as though he couldn't believe this was happening either, and got the hell off that bus where he belonged. Milly cringed as he stumbled past her. He headed hastily for home. The kids were still whooping it up in his honor. Half of them were already looking for Gordy. The bus suddenly lurched forward. Danny gave it the gun; he was fleeing the place.

Tom came up the front steps and into the hall.

He said, "The bus was early."

I turned and walked into the living room.

"It wouldn't have happened," he said, "if the bus had been on time. Is that the way to teach the kids punctuality?"

He followed me into the dining room.

"Maybe nobody noticed me."

He followed me into the kitchen.

"Yeah," he said dismally, "somebody noticed me. God, what am I going to say to Gordy?"

I picked up my purse and the car keys.

For centuries men, when things got less than enchanting at home, have had their corner saloons and their clubs. Now at long last we women, when life at home becomes unbearable, have something too. It's about time.

I parked the car, went through the self-swinging door and judiciously selected a basket cart. For almost an hour I escaped into a haze of hypnotic buying. As I wandered the aisles, bending my elbow to lift things from the shelves, having just one more here, just one more there, my troubles dissolved into a tipsy blur. A comforting numbness took me in its arms. When I discovered at the check-out counter that I had bought four large packages of instant tea, I didn't give a hoot. After all, that was only about thirty-five minutes of tea, if you kept at it. Loaded with lovely big brown paper bags, I staggered out into the world. Now I could face it.

A grim voice pierced my glow. "Emmy!"

I turned. "Hello, Milly."

"Well!" she said. "The end! This morning, the bus. The absolute end!"

In one second flat I was wet-hen mad again. "How right you are!" I said, seething. "The absolute end!"

"It's not just this morning," Milly said. "That was just the inevitable climax of the past weeks. He's been heading for something like this. I saw it coming. Inevitably. His not working, his drinking . . ."

"The swine!" I snapped.

"Emmy!"

"Yes!"

"This can't go on!"

"Not possibly!"

"It's got to stop!"

"Yes!"

"You must put your foot down!"

"At long last!"

"Take steps!"

"Drastic steps!"

"At once!"

"Immediately!"

"Or he'll drag you all down with him!"

"Yes! Good-by, Milly."

"Where are you going?"

"Put my foot down," I said, "and take steps!"

I jammed on the brakes and sent the gravel in the driveway flying. I slammed the car door and then frustration swept through me. Tom's car was gone. But there was another car parked in our drive. Harley Nicholson's Buick. Our leading real estate agent was paying the Wades one of his special, far-seeing calls. Well, Harley was right again.

He came around from behind the garage.

"Hello, Emmy," he said.

"Hello, Harley," I said.

"About an acre and a half, isn't there?"

"And three quarters."

"City water?"

"Artesian well."

"School bus stops in front of the . . . oh-oh, we won't go into that!"

"You know about it already?"

"It's all over town," Harley said, chuckling. "What a story!"

"Yes," I said. "Isn't it?"

Harley stopped chuckling and got back down to business. "How many bedrooms?"

"Two . . . no, three actually. There's a guest room."

"Baths?"

"One up, one down."

"What do the taxes run you?"

"Annually?"

Harley nodded.

"About five-seventy-five."

"How big a mortgage?"

"Almost down to thirteen thousand now."

"Who holds it?"

"Bridgeport Trust."

"Asking price?"

"Well, I want your advice on that."

"I haven't ever been through the house, Emmy . . ."

"Come right in."

I got through the morning by keeping very busy. First I made some of the necessary phone calls. Then I did the things that needed done immediately. After that I had time to divide the silver, on paper of course, the china, and the furniture. I didn't even bother to go into the guest room. There was no dividing to do in there. I kept so busy that I was

surprised that it was almost one-thirty when Tom got back.
"Sweetheart," he said, "listen . . ."
"I've reserved a room for you for tonight at the Three
Zebras," I said.
"What?"
"I've packed your bag."
"Emmy . . ."
"I hope you think forty-two-five is the right asking price.
Harley thought so."
"What the hell . . ."
"I've decided that you can have Gordy Labor Day, Thanks-
giving, Decoration Day, Father's Day and a week in August."
"Emmy, my God . . ."
"Of course you won't be able to pay any alimony. I'll get
a job. Macy's basement or maybe Gimbels' . . ."
"Darling, listen!"
"Just one other thing. Was that pearl-handled soup ladle
your grandmother's or mine?"
"Emmy!" Tom shouted. "Listen! I've solved our problem!"
"Your problem, not mine."
"I see my mistake, darling!"
"What?" I said. "You see your mistake?"
"Oh, God, how stupid I've been! I just realized what I
should do, Em, I've got the answer!"
"Tom . . . you're serious? You've come to your senses at
last?"
"Yes! I could kill myself for not realizing sooner."
"Darling," I said, "let's have a beer and you tell me all
about it."
"No beer," Tom said firmly. "No more of that stuff."
"Just one," I said. "To celebrate."
"All right," Tom said reluctantly. "Just one."

Chapter Thirteen

A whistle blew.

It sent a chill down my spine. Gordy didn't seem to hear it; he was sunk too deep in his despair. But for Tom it was obviously the sound he wanted to hear most in the world. His voice had a Christmas morning-New Year's Eve-Pay Day whoop in it.

"All ashore," he said, "that's going ashore!"

Milly Talbot stood up. She took both my hands in hers. She tried to speak, but now that all was irrevocably lost, she couldn't. She was only able to wag her head in acute sympathy.

"Thanks for the Dramamine," I said sadly.

"And thanks for the Kaopectate," Gordy said desolately.

"And thank Bob," Tom said sincerely, after taking a sip of sauerkraut juice, "for the six cans of sauerkraut juice."

Milly gave my hands a final, commiserating squeeze, patted a dismal farewell on the back of Gordy's bowed head, gave Tom a last furious look of disapproval and stumbled away.

"What a sourpuss," Lois Baker, a new friend of mine, said. "Cute cabin."

"Great, isn't it?" Tom said.

"Compact," I said.

"Easy to keep clean," Lois said. "Cute porthole. Have you seen the captain?"

"Not yet," Tom said.

"Probably shy. Beds look comfy."

"Beds?" I said.

"Bunks," Lois said. "They won't roll around. Harder to make, though. Cute life preservers. How many tons are you?"

"Twelve," Tom said.

"That's plenty," Lois said. "Wish I was going with you. Or else Fred and Charley were. Either them or me. Well, back to Foulfield County. Cook, cook, cook." She gulped down the remains of her drink. "Lousy champagne."

"Oh, no," I said. "Not at all. Thank Fred for sending it."

"He was afraid to bring it himself."

"Thank Charley for me," Gordy said, "for the Necco Wafers."

"I had to twist his arm to make him let go of them. Were there many gone?"

"Just a couple."

"Well, bon voyage," Lois said. "Good voyage."

Tom saw her graciously out into the corridor, or whatever you call it, shouting nauseous, nautical jocularities after her. Harley Nicholson stepped quickly out of the doorway to the bathroom, or whatever you call it. He had been wedged there by necessity for the duration of our gruesome gala. He made sure Gordy wasn't paying any attention, then said quietly, "Emmy, I really think you should let me put an "option to buy" clause in any rental lease I do for your house."

"No, Harley."

"You'll never make a go of it, you and Tom."

"We're going to try."

"Hopeless," Harley said. "Absolutely hopeless. I've been in real estate too long not to know."

Tom squeezed back into the cabin. He clapped Harley on the shoulder.

"Harley, old pal," he said, "great of you to see us off."

"Thanks for the flowers, Harley," I said.

"Thanks for the ball-point pen," Gordy said. "That address on it is your old office, isn't it?"

"Yes, well . . ." Harley looked around for someplace to put his full glass of champagne. He set it on Tom's suitcase. "Well, I better be going ashore," he said, and chuckled. "Of course, you've heard that story about Chet Cole, haven't you?"

Only Gordy said, listlessly, that he hadn't. Having rarely received that much encouragement, Harley beamed, licked his chops and was off, chuckling brilliantly.

"Well, you all know how Chet swore that if they put the Connecticut Turnpike through Darien, he'd never go out of his house again as long as he lived. Well, this was before that, when Chet was still getting out. This time he went down to New York to see the Barrows off to Paris on the old *Ile*. It was quite a bon voyage party, as you could well imagine if you knew Kitty and Red Barrow and Red's mother, who was going with them. The champagne flowed like the Mississippi. It was, as I said, quite a party. Well, the all-ashore sounded and everybody except Chet went ashore who was going ashore. So did Red's mother. They had to put her on a plane to Paris the next day. Well, there were Kitty and Red and Chet on the old *Ile* lapping up the champagne. Chet didn't have a passport, he only had the clothes on his back, and he was due at the office in Stamford that afternoon for something important. Chet loved good champagne and the Barrows could well afford the best. God, what a cheapskate that Fred Baker is. Well, Chet was having another and another and starting to yell about why didn't they widen the Merritt Parkway and the ship sailed. The old *Ile* took off with Chet on board. Later Kitty and Red said they thought Chet was Red's mother, which gives you some idea of how much champagne was flowing. There's nothing the slightest bit effeminate about Chet. He prides himself on that and he never spoke to Red or Kitty again. Come to think of it, Chet was in the wrong. There's nothing effeminate about Red's mother, either. But there was the old *Ile* headed for France and there was old Chet drinking and yakking away . . ."

"Harley," Tom said, "do you have a passport?"

". . . having the time of his life, not knowing that . . ."

"Harley," Tom said, "are those your only clothes?"

"What?"

"Are you due at the office?"

Tom pointed out the porthole.

"Oh, no!" Harley said.

"It's too far to jump," Tom said.

"Why, this sneaky little ship . . ."

"Might as well finish your story, Mr. Nicholson," Gordy said. "What happened to Chet?"

"They built the Turnpike through Darien," Tom said.

It cheered me a little to watch Harley climb ever so gingerly down the wobbling rope ladder after the harbor pilot and clamber into the rocking launch. We waved, but he didn't. He was looking anxiously toward the Sandy Hook Lightship, his next stop on his long way home.

The rope ladder was pulled up. Something grumbled down below us and the *Guy Fawkes* was churning toward Casablanca, then perhaps to the Canaries, then maybe to Tangier, then for sure, they said, to Málaga, which is about ten miles by land from Torremolinos, a Spanish village where a man and his family can live practically for nothing while the man is inspired by his new surroundings to write the novel he couldn't write in his old surroundings.

Never before had I appreciated to what a disadvantage loving somebody can put a person. One moment I thought I wanted to divorce him. The next I thought it wasn't stupid to yank Gordy out of school, rent our lovely house at the loveliest time of the year, and take off for a strange, hot, dry land famous for its seventeenth-century painting and plumbing so he can write a book you sometimes wonder if he will ever write, to put it mildly. Marrying a man you love, then spending twelve delightful years with him, sharing his bed, darning his socks, unfreezing his food, very possibly softens not only a girl's heart but her head. There could be no other explanation to how I became a party to this. At the moment I was as much annoyed with myself as I was with Tom.

Well, I had regained a husband. But I had, partially at least, lost a son. Gordy only spoke to me because he had to speak to someone in our family in order to find out where things were. He considered it treachery for me to have agreed to a plan that took him away from his friends and the Little League. This was going to have been his greatest season, in the field and at the plate. He was sure he was going to lead his team to a National Championship and attract the attention of a Yankee scout who was looking for someone to replace Mickey Mantle ten years from now. Gordy was bitter. Here he was, not in center field, but on a "dopey boat going to a dopey place where all they play is soccer. Soccer, Mom!"

I had to agree with him about the boat. Tom had been too enthusiastic about economizing. The *Guy Fawkes* was a tramp steamer and she was every inch a tramp. In fact, she looked downright seedy, if not a little leaky.

"Trim, isn't she?" Tom said.

A bell rang.

"Lunch," Tom said.

"No," I said. "The fare you paid couldn't possibly include meals."

Tom smiled the best he could. "Let's go! Come on, Gordy!"

"Mom," Gordy said, "I'm not hungry. If you want me, I'll be in my cell."

Tom said, "You've got to eat."

"Mom," Gordy said, "I'm seasick."

"You aren't," I said. "You couldn't be. Not yet."

"Well, then I've got . . . you know, what sailors get. Scurvy."

I laughed. Gordy had to laugh, too. Tom joined in our laughter. Gordy and I stopped laughing. We looked at Tom inquiringly. But we did go to lunch with him.

We were seated at the captain's table. The captain wasn't. Our waiter, or whatever you call him, one of a staff of two, explained that the master of the ship was too busy to eat.

Probably, I thought, supervising the bailing. The waiter then served thick, gray potato soup in thick, gray plates the size of Volkswagon wheels. I noticed immediately that we had the better waiter. He could carry two of these plates at once, smiling. The other could only manage one, frowning.

There were two tables, one for each waiter. At ours were two other seafaring adventurers, one a young man of about thirty, the other a distinguished, stern gentleman of maybe sixty. He ate his soup with precision. At the other table a group of five were introducing themselves to each other.

Tom broke our ice.

"We're the Wades," he said quite frankly. He pointed to me and said, "Emmy." He pointed to Gordy and said, "Gordy." He pointed to himself and darned if he didn't say, "Tom."

"Branton," the stern, distinguished gentleman snapped. His lips clicked together like heels. "E. P. Branton. Baltimore."

"I'm Ken Walters," the young man said. "Hi, Emmy. Hi, Gordy. Hi, Tom."

"Hi," we said, "Ken."

"Where are you going? Any certain place?"

"Spain," Tom said. "Torremolinos."

"Know it well. For how long?"

"Six months," Tom said. "Seven, eight."

"Oh," Ken said, "you're a writer."

"Why, yes!" Tom said, admiring Ken more and more. "How could you tell?"

"Yes," I said. "How could you?"

"Anyone going to Torremolinos for six or seven months is either a writer, artist, divorced or single. You have to be either a writer or an artist. I guessed writer. Had much published?"

"Well, no. Actually, nothing yet."

Ken nodded. "Torremolinos."

"Gordy," I said, "not so fast!"

"This soup's good!" Gordy said without slowing down.

"Ken," I said, "are you for or against Torremolinos?"

"It all depends. Did you ever happen to read *Bargain Spots*? Or *Around the World on a Dollar a Day*? Or *Retire on Next to Nothing*?"

"Oh," Tom said, "you're a writer, too. You wrote them."

"I wrote them, yes, but I don't call myself a writer, not really."

"Roving journalist," Tom said.

"Thanks," Ken said.

"Mr. Branton," Tom said politely, "where are you going?"

"Elba."

"Elba?" Ken said.

"Ken," Tom said, "now can you figure out what Mr. Branton is?"

"No," Ken said. "To tell the truth I know of only one person who ever went to Elba, and he didn't want to. Mr. Branton, what takes you to Elba?"

"This ship," E.P. snapped. "God willing."

The next course was great slabs of gray roast beef, gray mashed potatoes and small, greenish peas. The salad added the color. A slice of canned pineapple with half a canned peach on it, topped with a handful of maraschino cherries.

"Boy!" Gordy said. "Oh, boy!"

"Sure," Tom said. "The food's got to be good. We eat the same as the crew, and the seamen's union is the strongest there is."

"I believe you," I said.

"Ken," Tom said, "so this is a working trip for you, too."

Ken nodded. "I keep checking places and revising my books."

Tom nodded. "You have to keep up to date."

Ken nodded. "Up to the minute."

Tom nodded. "Sure, or else . . ."

While Tom and Ken cemented their friendship, I took a

better look at the passengers at the second table. Three of them seemed to have something in common. It wasn't a family resemblance, but they seemed related somehow. They were dapper, smooth. They kept shrugging their jacket collars more snugly up around their necks and straightening their bow ties and laughing in unison. They were in their early forties, but they looked collegiate. Cute, Lois would certainly have said. The other two passengers had their backs to me.

A certain feeling took me over before I knew it. I felt elated, excited even, and I didn't mind anymore that we were going on this ridiculous trip. I was smiling; I couldn't stop. My eyelashes were fluttering as they hadn't fluttered in years. My hands kept touching up my hair and I was worried about my lipstick but, darn it, I hadn't brought it with me. I didn't realize what was going on until Gordy explained it.

The waiter lowered dessert in front of Gordy. It was a quarter of an apple pie with nearly a pint of vanilla ice cream on it.

"Man!" Gordy said. "Oh, man, what a union!" Then he spoke to the waiter. "Hey, Mister, what's the cook's name?"

"Sam Gowdowski. Good, huh?"

"I'll say! Hey, Mom!"

"Yes, dear?"

"You're the only woman on board."

"Really? Well!"

I heard a humming, then soft singing in vintage harmony, the harmony of my salad days. It came from the next table. "'Time on my hands,'" the trio crooned, "'you in my arms . . .'"

They were singing to me. Who else?

I blushed.

Chapter Fourteen

"What's the name of that?" Tom asked.

"Name of what, dear?"

"That song you're humming."

"Was I humming?"

"You've been humming all afternoon."

"Really? I guess it's just a habit . . . while I do my nails and hair and . . . do you like my hair this way?"

"Well, yes, but . . . it's a little ingenue, isn't it?"

"Really? You really think it makes me look younger?"

"Em . . ."

"Yes, dear?"

"I don't believe . . . on freighters . . . you dress for dinner."

"This? You call this dressing?"

"Well, it's kind of . . . gay. Low-cut."

"It just happens to be the most comfortable thing I own."

"Okay."

We went on dressing for dinner.

Tom said, "What the hell is the name of that?"

"Oh. Humming again? Sorry. I wonder if we will stop at Casablanca and the Azores."

"It's possible, I'm afraid."

"That would add four or five days, wouldn't it?"

"Yeah."

I went into the bathroom to do my eyes. Tom said something I couldn't hear. "What, dear?"

" 'Time on My Hands.' That song you're humming."

"Oh . . . I will keep humming, won't I?"

"Em . . ."

"Yes, dear?"

"All that eyeshadow . . . this isn't the *Leonardo da Vinci*."

"No," I said. "But trim, isn't she?"

Dinner was a rich, thick, split-pea soup, a fine, big pot roast, and a surprisingly delicious rice pudding, just swimming with raisins and delightfully crowned with a scoop of raspberry jello. It did my heart good to see the men eat.

The captain couldn't have turned out to be more charming. He was English; he might have stepped right out of C. S. Forester. When I told him he reminded me, more than a little, of Captain Hornblower he, so typically, became all gruff and pretended never to have heard of anyone by that name.

After dinner we adjoined to the lounge for coffee. Steaming mugs of strong, black coffee with brimming pitchers of Carnation milk for those of us who wanted cream. The trio sang number after number, and Ken told some enchanting travel stories about trouble going through customs, getting locked in toilets in strange lands, things like that. The captain, Mr. Branton, and the two other gentlemen, whose names I didn't catch amid all the gaiety, played whist.

The evening simply flew by. Before I knew it all the men had gone to bed and I found myself alone in the lounge. I had three lovely cigarettes, writing in my mind the letter I'd send to Milly Talbot telling about everything. Then, on second thought, I decided to write it to Lois. Lois would appreciate it all more.

If only, I mused over my fourth filter-tip, Jackie Wilkins were here. Jackie was my roommate until she got kicked out sophomore year for inciting what in later years was to become known in academic circles as a panty raid by waving hers over graciously from our open dormitory window. They were empty, of course, but she got bounced anyway. Small school. Very well thought of, though. I guess they aimed to keep it that way.

After dances, parties, and dates Jackie and I used to sit up till dawn, reliving our evenings, dissecting, analyzing, and comparing our young men, dreaming and hoping, sighing and giggling, smoking and smoking. Quite often, in fact so often it finally got boring for me, we spent hour after hour weighing the possibility of Jackie's pregnancy. No, reconsidering, it was just as well Jackie was not aboard. Definitely. But definitely, as we used to say. Just me. Still, it would be fun to have a room-mate to share all this with . . .

Well, bed for me. A girl needed lots of sleep to look her best. I tidied up the lounge, stacked coffee mugs, emptied ash trays, plumped the pillow. I took a good-night look around the cozy little room . . . if we did stop at Casablanca and the Azores, it would last almost three weeks.

I tiptoed into our cabin, closed the door quietly and groped my way carefully toward the bathroom to undress.

Tom said, "You can turn the light on."

"I thought you'd be asleep."

"Not yet. Too much pot roast, I guess."

"Or coffee, maybe." I turned on the light. "Or excitement. Shall we have one last cigarette?"

"What?"

"Let's! I'll get undressed and in bed and we'll have one last cigarette and we'll talk! Shall we? Let's!"

"My God!" Tom said and, for some reason, laughed. "Yeah! Let's! Shall we?"

"All right!"

"All right! While you undress, I'll get the cigarettes going!"

In no time at all I was in my darling little bunk, my knees tucked up under my chin and puffing away. Tom blew a cloud of smoke at the ceiling, turned his head toward me and grinned.

"Hi!" I said.

"Hello, there!" Tom said.

"It was fun hearing all those old songs, wasn't it?"

"Wasn't it!"

"They're darling, those three! Len's the best looking, don't you think?"

"Len? Um . . . Fritz, I'd say."

"Well, maybe. Don has the nicest smile, though."

"He didn't smile at me. But I noticed how he kept smiling at you. All evening."

"You're exaggerating!"

"No!" Tom insisted. "All evening!"

"I just happened to be sitting where he was smiling. What's that fellow's name with the long sideburns?"

"Curly hair? Blue serge suit?"

"No, the baldish one, tweed jacket, black knit tie . . . played whist . . ."

"Oh, that one! Frank Cassini. I thought he was the best-looking one playing whist . . ."

"You did? Oh, Tom!"

"Well, maybe not."

"Oh, he's attractive, very virile, but . . ."

"Which one do you think?"

"I can't decide!"

"Take your time, we have all night."

"Well, the captain . . . there's something about him, not that he's actually handsome, but you know, something . . . then Mr. Branton . . ."

"Strong, silent type."

"Yes! He scares me! And the other one . . ."

"Phil Harding," Tom said. "Leslie Howard."

"Did you notice that, too?"

"Right away. And I noticed something else. How he kept looking at you."

"Oh, stop it! Was he really?"

"He came in last at whist. Em . . ."

"What?"

"Of all of them . . . which one would you rather be stranded on a desert island with?"

"Let's see." I lit another cigarette. "You know, Ken is really the best-looking . . . you mean just overnight or for a long period of time?"

"Oh, shut up and go to sleep."

"What?"

"Turn out the light, for God's sake!"

"Tom . . ."

"Mr. Branton scares you! Fun hearing those old songs! Cassini's virile! Don and his nice smile! Leslie Howard!"

"Tom, dear . . ."

"Listen, I've never seen a worse bunch of creeps and bores in my life! I thought we might get a few drips, but this! Good night!"

"Good night, darling," I said happily.

I drifted off into the most marvelous, gently sea-rocked sleep, safe in the knowledge that our bridge was manned by Captain Lanning. Then, too, in case of accident, there wouldn't be too much of a problem about women and children first.

The sun streaming through our adorable porthole woke me at five-thirty. I couldn't get back to sleep; I was smiling too much. Being careful not to wake Tom, I slipped out of bed and dressed quietly. First I put on black velvet slacks and a sweater. That seemed a bit ostentatious, perhaps even kind of obvious. I changed into a simple white blouse and a flamenco skirt. I sauntered out on deck, glanced casually about. No one was in sight. Not a soul. The ship seemed to be running itself, for heaven's sake. I strolled the deck.

Up front, in the prow part, I saw this little fellow sitting, alone and forlorn, on a heap of rope. His chin was on his fists, his elbows on his knees, and he was staring at the deck between his feet. He was wearing the new pajamas, bathrobe, and slippers he had got for his first trip abroad. I went and sat beside him. He pressed his lips into an even smaller, straighter line. I kissed him on the top of his head; it seemed to bristle to a point.

"You're up early," I said.

"So are you. Couldn't you sleep a wink either on this dopey boat?"

"I slept fine. And I looked in on you two or three times and you were sound asleep."

"I was?" Gordy asked, disgusted with himself.

"Yes, dead to the world."

"Oh, yeah, now I remember. Two or three times?"

"That's right."

"So rough. The dopey waves. Two or three times I got knocked unconscious."

"You were unconscious all right, but it was all that dinner you ate. Wonderful food, isn't it?" I asked casually.

Gordy looked at me with a suspicion that flared into resentful reproach. "Listen, Mom! I noticed something!"

"Yes, dear?"

"All of a sudden yesterday you got to like this dopey boat! You like everything now! Even Daddy!"

"Gordy . . ."

"Admit it! You even like Daddy again!"

"All right," I said defiantly, "I'm not ashamed to admit it. I do like him again."

"Oh, brother! Never trust a woman! Well, listen . . . where does that leave me?"

"Leave you?"

"Yeah . . . is it all right if I like him again?"

"I think it might be all right. If you really mean it, it might be nice."

"After all, what he did, was that so terrible?" Gordy demanded. "He got on the bus to say good-by to me! Is it so terrible to want to say good-by to your kid? Your only kid?"

Then in a small voice Gordy said, "Gee . . ."

"What?"

"It was terrible, wasn't it?"

"Well . . . not all that bad."

"No! And the other stuff . . ."

"Past history."

"Yeah! And taking me out of school, I'm willing to forgive him for that. To tell the truth, I always have been."

"Traveling is an education. And your baseball, is that so important?"

"Well . . ."

"Look at it this way. Maybe a season away from the game will do you a lot of good."

"Might it?"

"You're young . . ."

"Yeah, I am young. Ten and a half."

"So!"

"Okay! But . . ."

"But what?"

"I can't just start talking to Daddy all of a sudden."

"Why not?"

"What will I say to him?"

"You'll think of something."

"Maybe I'll wait till tomorrow."

"Write him a letter, why don't you?"

"Where would I mail it?"

"Slip it under his door."

"Seems sneaky . . ."

"Hi," Tom said. "Good morning."

Gordy stood up and faced his father. His hands closed into fists. He was breathing hard. Tom looked at him in surprise, then looked at me.

I said, "Gordy has something to say to you."

Tom turned back to Gordy. Gordy looked as if he might dive overboard. He stood there, gulping. Then he began to yell.

"Last of the ninth . . . tie score . . . two out . . . you're up, Pop!"

"I dig in," Tom said.

"I throw you a low curve on the outside . . . you get ahold of it . . . there it goes . . . headed for the stands . . ."

"It's fair all the way," I said.

"A home run, Pop! You did it!"

"Boy!" Tom said.

"Boy, oh, boy!" Gordy said. "Hey, I better get dressed for breakfast. I don't want to be late. Want to see my cabin?"

"Yeah," Tom said.

"C'mon! It's neat!"

Chapter Fifteen

It was late. We were amazed at how late it had gotten. It had been hours since Tom had gone off to bed with Strunk and White's *Elements of Style,* leaving us in the lounge together. When I next looked at my watch, we couldn't believe it was almost three. We had gone out on deck for a last look at the moon together. Now we tiptoed down the corridor to my cabin. We were very careful not to waken Tom. We whispered our good nights.

"Good night, Emmy."

"Good night, Ken."

"Good night, Emmy."

"Good night, Fritz."

"Good night, Emmy."

"Good night, Don. Good night, Len."

"Good night, my dear."

"Good night, Phil."

"Good night, Mrs. Wade."

"Good night, Mr. Cassini."

They stole away, smiling and waving over their shoulders. Carefully, quietly, I opened the door. I didn't waken Tom. He was standing in the middle of the cabin, putting on his shirt. When he saw me he stopped putting it on. He was cross; he was very, very cross. Strunk and White's *The Elements of Style* lay awkwardly in a corner where he had obviously, angrily, thrown it. Furtively, I picked it up, eyes averted.

"Where in the hell," Tom demanded, ripping off his shirt, "have you been?"

"Please," I pleaded, "keep your shirt on."

"My God! I was beginning to wonder if you'd fallen overboard. I was coming to see."

"You and your morbid curiosity."

"What the hell was all that rustling out there just now? It sounded like the rats were deserting the ship."

"Those were not rats," I said loyally. "They happen to be a group of my friends seeing me safely home."

"A group, for God's sake! How many?"

"You keep count. Len and Fritz and Don and Ken . . . am I going too fast? And Phil Harding and . . . oh, yes, Mr. Cassini."

"Where the hell were the captain and the crew? Tied up?"

"If you're going to be sarcastic, Tom," I said quietly, putting Strunk and White's *The Elements of Style* down on top of Fowler's *The King's English*, "I won't tell you what went tonight with me and the fellows."

"The hell you won't, I'll bet you will! You're dying the hell to!"

"Stop swearing! Darling, I'm not jealous of Strunk and Fowler, E. B. White, and Bergen Evans, so I don't see why you should be jealous of Don, Fritz and Len, Phil Harding and . . ."

"Please!"

"Ken and Mr. Cassini."

Tom got into his bunk and pulled the covers over his head. But only for a moment. "Why the mister?" he asked, delighted with his sarcasm. "Mr. Cassini. Did you two tiff?"

I chose to ignore his sarcasm.

"No, Tom, now that you ask, and I'm glad you ask, we just don't seem to have got very close, Mr. Cassini and I. Mr. Cassini's quiet. Reserved. Oh, we're friends, yes, but . . . how shall I say it? You know, actually . . . well, now that you've brought it up, it's a curious thing."

I lit two cigarettes, gave one to Tom. He groaned, but I chose to ignore that, too. "Actually, Tom, I don't really know any of them. We've spent hours together. Collectively, you might say, we're friends, but, individually, you ask? No, Tom, not really."

"Emmy?"

"Yes, dear?"

"What did you drink?"

"Phil Harding brought a bottle of kirsch up from his cabin."

"Did Phil and the other fellows get any of it?"

"We shared and shared alike. They had half and I had half. Actually, it was cute. They each drank a toast to me and I each drank a toast to each of them. No, Tom, actually, I haven't had a moment alone with a single one of the fellows. It's always been all of us together. Our conversation has been . . . how shall I say it? General? Conceivably, yes. Actually, I'd like to get to know them. Who are they? What are they? What do they want? Why don't you have some sauerkraut juice and I'll just finish up this little bit of sherry while I'm at it. No? Where are they going? Oh, I don't mean on this ship . . . their lives. Here we are all of us . . . three days ago we didn't know each other existed . . . merely existed . . . and now suddenly here we are thrown together. But who are we, really? Oh, we're all charming . . . each in our own way . . . and exciting . . . but there's more to us than that . . . down deep we're people and I want to get to know us, each of us, to find the splendid secret me inside all of us . . . Tom . . . Tom, dear . . ."

I took the cigarette from between his fingers.

The captain, in his beautifully tailored tan sailor suit, looked jaunty, ever so nautical and terribly alone. I joined him at the rail. His eyes in his lean, salted face were crinkled as they scanned his friend and enemy, the sea.

"Good morning, Captain!"

"Couldn't sleep, eh?" he asked with his pretended gruff-ness.

"I don't want to miss a moment of this! Breath-taking . . . so . . . so vast! Is that a speck on the horizon?"

But the captain was peering down into our wake.

"What is it, Captain?"

"Looks deep, doesn't it?" he said uneasily.

"Why, yes, it does, sort of. How deep would you say it was?"

"Hate to know." He turned his back to the rail. "Deep enough."

"I hope I'm not . . . I mean don't let me keep you from the bridge."

He glanced up at it. "Probably somebody or other up there."

"Have you always known the sea, Captain?"

"Huh?"

"Have you always . . . you know . . . worked on a boat?"

He blew, in reply, his nose on a beautifully tailored blue bandana.

"How many sister ships does the *Guy Fawkes* have, Cap-tain?"

"Sister what?"

"Ships. You know."

"Two," he said expansively.

"Really? Where are they? Do you happen to know?"

"Know exactly. The *Deep Blue* is off Malta."

"Malta!"

"Two miles off Malta. At the bottom of the Mediterranean. All hands lost. The *Blue Horizon* is on the rocks off Orkney. No survivors."

"Oh," I said. "Don't you think . . . this is just a suggestion, but shouldn't we maybe have a life-boat drill?"

The captain looked at me distastefully. "No use inviting trouble."

"Well, couldn't we at least run through 'Nearer My God to Thee' once or twice?"

"Never could stand that piece. Gloomy."

"How about 'Abide with Me' then? You know, with the trio aboard we could have a really lovely sinking." The captain turned to look at me again; quickly, I said, "But let's talk about you. What drew you to the . . ."

The captain hurried away.

In a moment Mr. Branton came marching stiffly, resolutely along the deck, his dark eyes brooding beside his fierce, hawklike nose. The mystery of this restless, bitter man intrigued me more and more each day. I smiled at him.

"Good morning, Mr. Branton!"

He nodded, but not enough to wrinkle his neck.

"Join me at the rail, won't you?"

"Thank you very much," he snapped, "but I'm late."

"Late? For what, for heaven's sake?"

He was so far away I couldn't hear whether he answered or not.

"Hi, Mom!"

"Oh. Hi."

"Did I say something wrong?"

Far off in the moonlight I could see the gray, graceless silhouette of another freighter beating its way westward, ho, carrying the wines of France to the New World. Gin and tonic from England, Danish pastry, Scotch tape. Or maybe it was just returning empty Coca-Cola bottles. We were carrying mainly cake mix to the Old World. If we sank there would be the biggest cake ever on the bottom of the Atlantic.

Behind me in the lounge I could hear the trio enjoying its special medley of "Violets" (Sigma Alpha Epsilon), "Smoke Dreams" (Phi Gamma Delta) and "Sweetheart of Sigma Chi" (Sigma Chi). Tom was in our cabin reading the Bible to improve his style. Gordy was in his bunk sleeping, killing time until breakfast.

I had slipped away from our gang in the lounge, pleading a slight headache and the need of some fresh air. This was a delusion and a snare, in that order. I hoped that one of the boys, any one but just one, would follow me out and we would have a talk. As I had explained to Tom the night before, it was a shame that we weren't getting to know each other, what we believed in, stood for, dreamed of . . .

"Emmy, my dear," Phil Harding said.

"Phil," I said.

"How's your head?"

"Better. Divine night, isn't it? The moon, the stars, the sea. What does it all mean, Phil? What does it mean to you?"

He didn't answer immediately. The fine line of his delicate, sensitive profile turned away from the moon, the stars, the sea, to me. The long, slender fingers of his artist's hands touched my face and turned it to him. He looked deeply, intently into my eyes. At last he spoke, his voice gentle, anxious.

"Are you sure, my dear, you're not constipated?"

"What?"

"Your eyes look rather liverish. This food, you know, would kill a horse. And your headache . . . nature's warning, you know. Here, take this."

"Phil, I . . ."

"No, no, I insist. You needn't be afraid of it. It isn't habit forming. You'll be regular in a jiffy. My doctor gives me a prescription. I never travel without it. Are you getting enough exercise?"

"Well, I . . ."

"I'm sure you're not! Come along, we'll do thirty around the deck. No, no, don't talk . . . no talking . . . just breathe deeply . . . in and out . . ."

When I limped into the cabin, Tom was sound asleep.

I didn't waken him to tell him about my evening. I took the Bible off his chest. His style hadn't been improved much yet. He was still in the "begats."

"Emmy, I've been hoping to talk to you alone."

"Have you really, Ken?"

"Yes, but you're in such demand . . ."

"Oh, no! Divine night, isn't it?"

"Beautiful! Emmy . . ." Ken said, and hesitated.

"What, Ken?"

"Well, I don't know how to say this . . ."

"Are we friends or aren't we, Ken?"

"I certainly hope we are."

"We are, Ken."

"Emmy, you're the most understanding person I've met for a long, long time. Please don't think I would come to just anybody . . ."

"Ken, you needn't explain. You know I'll understand, really will."

"Emmy, I need help," Ken said simply.

"I thought you might. I didn't think you were the confident, completely assured person you seem to be on the surface . . ."

"Things haven't been going well with me."

"At some time or other," I said sympathetically, "that happens to everybody. And that's the time you should turn to your friends . . ."

"I hoped you'd say that, Emmy." He put his hands gratefully on my shoulders. "And I hope this will be just between us. Tom won't have to know?"

"Just between us, Ken."

"Good," Ken said briskly. "I'll pay you back as soon as I can."

"What?"

"A couple of hundred will see me through . . ."

I caught Mr. Branton one twilight way up in the pointy part of the boat. He couldn't get past me without knocking me down; I had him trapped. He was peering far, far into the distance, searching for something, something he seemed hopeless of ever finding. His emperor's face was a mask of despair. His shoulders sagged; they were sagging so much I was afraid his coat would slide off them and down to the bottom of the pitiless sea. If ever a man needed help, a friend to talk to . . .

"Mr. Branton," I said.

I scared him; he jumped.

"I'm sorry," I said.

"Apology," he said, "accepted. Nice talking to you, and now if you'll excuse me . . ."

"Mr. Branton," I said, "may I ask you a question?" I saw the answer forming on his lips. Quickly, I said, "What's eating you? I mean . . . something seems to be troubling you. Perhaps if you . . . have you ever told anyone? Perhaps if you told me now . . . what is it that tortures you, Mr. Branton? What is this thing?"

He looked at me for a long time, then he turned away, but he spoke. Quietly, tonelessly, he said, "I broke my mother's heart."

After a moment I said, "Mr. Branton, how can we be sure that we have ever really broken anyone's heart?"

"Mother told me." The words came in a rush. "One of her great grandfathers fought for the British at Saratoga, another at Trenton for the Colonies. She had a grandfather at New Orleans under Jackson in the War of 1812. Her father and two uncles were in the Civil War. She had a husband, a brother, three cousins in the Spanish-American War. Then I came along, her only son, and I . . ."

"And you, Mr. Branton?"

"I flunked out of Staunton Military Academy."

"Oh, Mr. Branton . . ."

"I didn't get into West Point."

"Oh, Mr. Branton . . ."

"I would have been in Ike's class."

I watched him march slowly away.

"Please," Mr. Cassini said shyly, "call me Frank."

"And you call me Emmy, Frank."

"Thank you . . . Emmy."

"Don't mention it, Frank. Well, that certainly took a long time. Why are you so shy, Frank?"

"I've always been . . . around . . ."

"Louder, please, Frank, I can't hear you."

"Around ladies."

"You're not married, are you?"

"No . . . I . . ." Frank floundered painfully.

"You would rather not talk about it. All right, we'll talk of something else. Somebody said you were from Newark."

"I was born there. A Caesarian."

"A what . . . oh, yes, I see."

"You live in Westport, Connecticut, that right?"

"Near there."

"Is it true what they say about Westport?"

"What do they say?"

"You know."

"No, I don't, Frank."

"Well . . . some pretty wild times up there . . . wild parties . . . you know . . ."

"I can't hear you, Frank."

"Wife-trading!" Frank said loudly. "I understand," his voice dropped again, "there's a lot of that goes on Saturday nights."

"Not any more than any other night. Frank, let's talk about . . ."

"But it exists, that right? You still find some."

"No, it's dying out. Are you a baseball fan?"

"You ever see any, the wife-trading?"

"Why, yes! Yes, I have, Frank! Two fellows just down the road!"

"Traded, huh?"

"Yes! This Saturday night one fellow loaned the other his wife . . ."

"And the first one got the other's wife, go on . . ."

"No, the other one wasn't married."

"Wasn't married!"

"No, he loaned the first one his power lawn mower for three hours on Sunday morning. Good night, Mr. Cassini."

The ship was about halfway between Casablanca and the Azores. The gang was in the lounge, the trio in full swing. I wasn't sure where Tom was. Gordy was in his cabin, sleeping. I was in our cabin, reading Roget's Thesaurus. I had read everything else on board.

Tom came bouncing in.

"Em, come on, we're having a great time!"

"That bunch of creeps!"

"Look, if you really got to know them, really know them . . ."

I threw Roget's Thesaurus at him.

"Don't be such a drag, Em. You've hardly been out of this cabin for days . . ."

"The less I see of this miserable, dopey boat . . . my God, taking Gordy out of school, dragging us across the ocean . . ."

"Come on, Em, Phil Harding brought a bottle of kümmel up from his cabin . . . come on, join us . . ."

"No! I feel lousy! I'm constipated!"

"At least come and listen to us do 'Stardust' . . ."

"Us!"

"Yeah! We're a quartet now . . ."

I buried my face in the pillow, sobbed.

"Gordy Wade!" Ralph yelled hysterically. "This is your life!"

"Mine?" Gordy gasped.

"We fooled you all right, didn't we, Gordy? Ladies and gentlemen, we told Gordy he was being brought out here to California to be questioned by the Los Angeles police about holding up a gas station. Gordy, you're seventeen now, just about to graduate from high school and become eligible to sign a fat contract with the New York Yankees, plus a hundred thousand dollar bonus. You're going to take Mickey Mantle's place. Yes, Gordy, this is your life and what a life! Listen, Gordy!"

A voice from somewhere said, "I've known Gordy for seventeen years and Gordy was always a good boy, if I do say it myself . . ."

"Mom!"

I rushed out on stage and hugged Gordy.

"Where's Daddy?" Gordy asked.

"He's being questioned by the Los Angeles police about holding up a gas station."

"Gordy," Ralph said, "he'll be at the party in your honor at the Biltmore Hotel. Your father never missed a party in his life. Listen, Gordy!"

A voice said, "I knew Gordy would make it. Even as a little boy he would rather play baseball than eat . . ."

"Mom!"

"No, dear, I'm here."

"Coach!"

"Yes!" Ralph said. "Your Little League coach! Mr. Harley Nicholson!"

"I'm sure," Harley said, "you all have heard the story about the time . . ."

Ralph said, "Sit over there, Nicholson. Gordy, listen!"

A voice said, "I've been watching Gordy for eight, nine

seasons. Never saw him throw to the wrong base or go for a bad pitch. The kid's a natural . . ."

"Scout!"

"Yes, Gordy!" Ralph said. "The man who scouted you for the Yankees and he'll be the proudest man in the world next Tuesday when you graduate and sign your contract to play . . ."

A voice said, "Just a moment. Gordy can't sign any contract . . ."

"Principal!"

"Who?" Ralph asked.

"My high school principal!"

"Sorry, Gordy," the principal said, "but you're not graduating this June. That year in Spain . . . you never caught up . . ."

Chapter Sixteen

"*Senorita*," I said, "this thing isn't working."

The senorita smiled and nodded happily.

This didn't surprise me. We had read all the books on Spain our friends could find. The Galicians up there in the north, Atlantic corner of the Iberian Peninsula are deeply melancholy. Their towns smell of fish. But the Andalusians down here on the sun-soaked shore of the Mediterranean laugh and laugh. They are wits, practical jokers, poets, and singers. They talk all the time about fiesta, bulls, and women. There are, according to V. S. Pritchett, vestiges of harem life in Andalusia. When Gordy read that, his dirty little mind ran riot. "Hey, Mom," he yelled clear across the room, embarrassing me in front of my husband, "what are vestiges?" I made him look it up in the dictionary and he was terribly disappointed.

"*Senorita*," I said loudly, distinctly, "*el* thing. She does not work. No okay. Now hot. Now cold."

The senorita laughed and laughed and bobbed her pretty head merrily. If I hadn't known she was the child of a scented and voluptuous clime full of practical jokers and once enjoyed by the Moors, whose kingdom lasted more than (according to Pritchett) six hundred years, I would have thought this was her last day at work because she was getting married tomorrow morning and she didn't give a damn whether my hair ever dried. I took a deep breath to try my luck with the senorita again, but a raucous American voice two dryers down hollered something in Spanish. It galvanized the senorita. She slapped the dryer until my ears rang, she pulled out plugs, put them back in upside down, threw switches back and forth and had a wonderful time generally until my dryer resumed its noisy hum. Then she doubled up with glee and ran away. This was all too droll, apparently, to keep from her Andalusian friends, although it wouldn't have got a snicker out of a Galician whose town smelled of fish.

"Hey, number two," the raucous voice said, "can you hear me?"

"You're coming in fine, number four," I hollered back. "Over."

"How long have you been here? Over."

"We just got off our ship two hours ago."

"Where did you come from?"

"New York. By slow freight."

"Oh, Gawd. Do you live in New York?"

"Not quite. Connecticut."

"Westport?"

"Near there. Where do you live?"

"Here now," Number four hollered. "Monterojo."

"We're going to Torremolinos."

"That's on the other side of Málaga from us."

"Where did you live back home?"

"Everywhere, but I'm from Oregon."

"Really? I went to school in Oregon."

"My Gawd. Where?"

"A little college near Corvalis. Rogers and Clark."

"My Gawd. So did I!"

"Oh, no! When?"

"So long ago I can't remember."

"Me, too. Where are you from in Oregon?"

"Bend."

"Oh, no!" I said. "My roommate was from Bend!"

"My Gawd. Where are you from?"

"Akron, Ohio."

"I had a roommate from Akron!"

"Oh, no!"

"Emmy!" Number four screamed. "Is it you?"

"Jackie!" I screamed. "Is it you?"

The Spanish lady under dryer number three got her legs out of the way just in time. We met there.

"Well," Jackie said, "I'll be gawddamned."

"Jackie," I said, "are you pregnant?"

"Emmy! I don't know!"

"Jackie! It is you!"

"Emmy, my Gawd . . . are you married?"

"Yes!" I said. "Are you?"

"No! Not just now."

"Oh. Your marriage didn't work out?"

"None of them did, dammit. Look, we can't talk here . . ."

After Jackie got kicked out of Rogers and Clark she got kicked out of Pomona College (smoking), the University of Southern California (drinking) and the University of Arizona (subversion). While she was taking a course in speedwriting at a secretarial school in Los Angeles she met her first husband, a used car dealer with curly hair. It was a quick romance, so quick that Jackie didn't realize until after the wedding that her husband, habitually, didn't smoke, drink, or stay up late.

"My Gawd," Jackie said to me in the lobby of our hotel, "that's no basis for a happy marriage. Hey . . . *Camarero, dos mas!*"

"No more for me, Jackie, it's ten o'clock in the morning!"

"That late? Well, I can catch up if I hurry. *Camarero, dos mas para mi!*"

Jackie met her second husband, a Chicago subcontractor with curly hair while watching some excavating near the Adler Planetarium. This marriage lasted six months; they waited until the baby was born. Clifford, now fourteen, was with his mother in Monterojo.

"Does Clifford have curly hair?" I asked.

"My Gawd, you know I've no idea! I've always kept him in a crew cut. It might be interesting to see some day although, frankly, if I never see any more curly hair as long as I live it's all right with me."

Her next husband was the Schweppes distributor for Harrisburg and central Pennsylvania. That marriage lasted six years, mainly because Jackie kept thinking she was pregnant, partly because they didn't see much of each other. Jackie was away from home a lot. His dominating, interfering mother finally broke it up. There she was on the doorstep, Jackie said, every gawddam Christmas. Her last husband, whom she met at a sales convention, was the Schweppes distributor for Dade County, Florida.

"What broke up that one?" I asked.

"I don't know," Jackie sighed. "Nothing special. I guess some men just aren't suited for marriage."

I nodded sympathetically and said, "How do you happen to be living in Spain?"

"I rode over on a boat with a fellow who wanted to get away from his wife for a while and think things out."

"What did he finally think?"

"I often wonder. I met this crazy kid on the boat. His father gave him a motorcycle for not smoking until he was twenty-one. We shared expenses from Lisbon to Torremolinos."

"A motorcycle," I said, feeling relieved, but stuffy. "Then Clifford wasn't with you and . . . the fellows."

"No. He spends six months with his father in Chicago and I have him on my hands six months."

"Isn't that rough on Clifford's education?"

"It works out fine. He's been going to boarding schools around Chicago and it's never more than six months before he gets kicked out of them. You know," Jackie said, realizing something for the first time and glowing with parental pride over it, "he's only fourteen and he's been to at least as many schools as I ever went to."

"Jackie, is the school at Torremolinos good?"

"Very good. Clifford loved it."

"Oh," I said, worried.

"Why are you going to Torremolinos anyway? You're nuts!"

"We've heard it was inexpensive but interesting. We have to economize until Tom finishes his book."

"It isn't inexpensive anymore and what do you call interesting?"

"Well, the people . . ."

"Hi, Mom!"

"Gordy . . . Tom, the most amazing thing! I want you to meet Jackie Wilkins, she's an old roommate of mine! We just happened to find each other in the beauty shop."

"Gee!" Gordy said. "It's a small world!"

"Aw, Gordy," Tom said, "that's what I was going to say."

"Really?" Gordy said, even more awed. "It sure is a small world, isn't it?"

Jackie said, "What grade are you in, Gordy?"

"Fifth."

"So is Clifford. It'll be nice him knowing somebody in the same grade. All the kids his age are in junior high. Hello, Tom, I'm glad to meet you, but are you a nut or somebody? Going to Torremolinos?"

"Jackie says," I said, "that Torremolinos isn't inexpensive anymore."

"My Gawd!" Jackie said. "You know what a bottle of gin costs you there now?"

"No," Gordy said frankly.

"Forty-five pesetas!" Jackie told him indignantly.

"Holy smokes!" Gordy said, aghast.

"Forty-five pesetas," Tom said. "That's seventy-five cents."

"Yes! The gougers! And everything else has gone up proportionately . . . food, rents, maids . . . a maid costs you fourteen dollars a month!"

"A month!" I said.

"A month! The robbers! And they're off almost all day every Sunday. But that isn't all! The people! Tourists! Rich Swedes and Germans. The place is ruined. They have a traffic cop and a garbage man and a dog catcher. They're putting windows in the stores. You can get Kleenex! And Metrecal! There's a Berlitz school! And the new hotels! Every Spanish kid under sixteen is in uniform. Bellhops! Their hero used to be Manolete. Now it's Conrad Hilton. Stay away from there."

Tom said, "But aren't there still a lot of American writers and . . ."

"No! A few maybe. The Swedes and Germans take pictures of any they find. Oh, there are the television writers. They ride around in big Citroëns and play golf in the afternoon. They have agents and electric typewriters. Their wives go to Berlitz. After three weeks . . . they all go three weeks . . . they can count up to ten and ask their maids how they are. Listen, you come to Monterojo. It hasn't been discovered yet. The real writers and artists are there. Say, I know the most beautiful house for thirty-five dollars a month. Roger Simpson and Adele are just moving out. He's going back to London. Adele could break his neck. Here they were, the happiest couple in Monterojo, and the minute his wife's father dies and leaves her a lot of money, he walks out on Adele and goes back to his wife. We had a farewell party last night and Adele got sentimental and kept drinking toasts to Roger and throwing the glasses at his head, so there's a lot of broken glass all over the place, but . . ."

We stood on our balcony and looked at our view. Behind us in our living room our maid was sweeping up broken glass for ten dollars a month, plus room, plus board. She sang as she worked, or perhaps more accurately, she worked as she sang. The tinkling of the glass was a charming but casual background to her strenuous, all-out Flamenco. Her name was Isobelita Cabrera Fernandez. She was twenty-two. She was unmarried, but she didn't look as though that could go on much longer, or else the boys around here all married for money. A stunning girl, Senorita Isobelita Cabrera Fernandez.

"Tom," I said, "Gordy, look at the view!"

Our villa was halfway up a terraced cliff that soared majestically up from the golden beach of the blue Mediterranean. Above us, below us, and all around us were sparkling white little houses, nestling in an avalanche of flowers. Gay bougainvillaea, saucy carnations, obese, lazy roses, sweet-scented jasmine, justifiably conceited poinsettias, full moonflowers, raging vines of geraniums, to name a few. In little courtyards we could see orange, lemon, palm, and fig trees. We had only a eucalyptus in ours. It was blooming. Down on the golden beach a string of seven pretty burros were marching along, loaded with sand. Their bells rang. A woman in a red dress with a basket of white wash on her head climbed up the zigzag path of alternating steps and inclines that Romans once had used to scale the cliff to build the watchtower on the brink above us. Beyond it the early evening sun tamed the ancient, angry mountains and gave them a soft, opalescent coat of many colors. Beyond them the snow mountains of Granada, where once the Moorish princes . . .

"Mom!" Gordy yelled. "Hey, Mom, come to!"

"What, dear? Oh . . . sorry. It's . . . spellbinding, isn't it? Inspiring?"

"Yes," Tom said. He put one arm around me, the other around Gordy. "Monterojo. Spain."

"Heaven," I said. "It's heaven."

"It's too good for angels," Tom said.

"It's where angels go," I said, "when they die."

Isobelita screamed.

We turned and saw her indignantly rubbing her fanny and glowering at a stocky, almost squat figure sauntering toward us. He was wearing a plaid shirt with a button-down collar. His tie was early Countess Mara. He had on a Madras jacket, Bermuda walking shorts. His shoes were double-soled suede. He seemed to be smoking a cigar.

"Clifford," I said, without any hesitation or doubt.

"Welcome," Clifford said, his voice rasping, "to Stinkville."

"Clifford," Tom said, "please don't pinch our maid. Pinch your own maid."

"We don't have maids anymore."

None of us evinced surprise.

"Were you my mother's roommate?" Clifford said to me. "Or you?" he said to Tom.

"Now, Clifford," I said. "It was nice of you to call. This is a beautiful place your mother found us."

"This whole place is gonna fall off," Clifford said, beaming. "This whole cliff is gonna fall right off on its face."

"How do you know?" Gordy said.

"The rock is rotten. All the rock in Spain is rotten. Stinkville needs all new rock. Your name's Gordy, huh?"

"So what, huh?"

"I want to talk to you a minute."

He took Gordy over to the other end of the terrace. He pulled out what looked like a half a deck of playing cards from his pocket. He riffled them expertly for Gordy to see; Gordy's eyes popped.

"Ten pesetas for the first three days," Clifford said. "Five pesetas a day after that."

"Gordy," I called, "what are those?"

"Naked people!"

"Clifford!" I said.

"It's all right, Mrs. Wade," Clifford said. "I got different sets. This set is for Gordy's age group."

Chapter Seventeen

Tom got up early the next morning to catch the first bus to Málaga; he wanted to change our address at American Express from Torremolinos to Monterojo, find a friendly bank, and clean up all the details of settling down. He was anxious to get to work. What a place to write! "My God!" he said. "No wonder *Don Quixote* is so long!"

I had trouble getting back to sleep after Tom left. In a mirror on our bedroom wall I could see fishermen, some in three small boats, some on shore, bringing in a net. A burro, blindfolded so he wouldn't get dizzy, poor little thing, was helping by winding a windlass. The net looked heavy, a fine haul. The women of Monterojo would sing today. I could hear one already, far away. She sang me back to sleep.

Isobelita sang me awake.

I found Gordy on the balcony. He was wearing just his swimming trunks. He was reclining in a wicker chaise as he partook of his breakfast. Isobelita was attending him. She was piling, alternately, orange marmalade and strawberry jam on little circles of toast and delivering them to him, each with a devastating smile.

"*Muchas gracias, senorita,*" he kept saying, his mouth full of succulent toast.

"*De nada,*" she kept saying, her mouth full of beautiful teeth.

Finally, I used most of the Spanish I knew. "*Buenos dias,*" I said.

"*Buenos días,* Mom," Gordy said, without rising.

"*Buenos días, senora,*" Isobelita said.

That's all she said, those three words, but never in my

life have I felt so welcome. She made me feel as though she had known me for thirty years and hadn't seen me for twenty. Then she rushed off to the kitchen to get my coffee, as though it were serum to save my life. I sat down in a daze of delight.

Gordy sighed, clasped his hands behind his head, closed his eyes and held his face up to the sun. He said, "Those poor creeps."

"What, dear?"

He looked at his watch without opening his eyes. "About now they're going out of arithmetic single file like a bunch of prisoners on their way to spelling . . ."

"Now, now," Mother said, "none of that!"

"Boy, am I lucky!"

"Young man, you're going to school. An American school opened here last fall."

"I know," Gordy said, smiling.

"Exactly what do you know? Obviously, something I don't."

"They don't have any books yet for the fifth grade."

"Well, they can soon get some, can't they?"

"Not too soon. Clifford volunteered to write his father to send some."

When you speak of the devil he usually arrives pretty promptly. But not Clifford. He didn't show up until almost noon. He was wearing a male bikini, rope sandals, prescription sunglasses, and a white polo cap. He was carrying a portable radio, a thermos Coca-Cola bag, a full set of skin-diving equipment and a copy of *Playboy*. He smelled expensive.

"Hello, Clifford," I said. "Yardley's?"

"English Leather."

"Do you shave?" Gordy asked.

"No," Clifford said, "not yet. This isn't after-shaving lotion. You can use it before."

"Two years before," I said. "That's pretty good stuff. Where's your mother?"

"She's coming. Want to go to the lousy beach with us?"

"Sounds great," I said. "Clifford, have you written to your father lately?"

Clifford glanced disapprovingly at Gordy, then smiled an oily smile at me. "I write him every Sunday I get a chance. But it's a big waste of time. He can't read my writing. Nobody can," he added proudly.

"Hello," Jackie said. "You got any aspirin?"

"Yes," I said. "Is it bad?"

"Fierce. I sat up all night with Adele."

"Adele . . . oh, yes. The one who lived here, the sentimental one."

"She's suicidal."

"Oh, come on . . . really?"

"Really! She admits it. She says she's going to drink herself to death."

"On her alimony?" Clifford said derisively.

"I never would have thought of that," Jackie said admiringly. "She can only drink champagne. Anything else makes her sick at her stomach and if I know Adele she'd rather be alive than sick at her stomach."

"I'll bump her off for thirty-five dollars."

"Clifford! You're not to say things like that. If you need money, ask for it. You'll meet Adele tonight," Jackie said to me, "at the party. Skip Cole sold a story and got his check. We're all going down to celebrate. At his place. I'll pick you and Tom up about ten. Where the hell's that aspirin?"

"Come with me."

Jackie followed me into the bedroom. "You'll meet all the writers and everybody. It's going to be some party. This is Skip's first sale in a year and a half. Thanks. Three more. Skip went over to Gib . . ."

"Gib?"

"Gibraltar to get some scotch. I wonder if Adele can keep scotch down."

"Jackie, you chew aspirin!"

"It's such a bore always getting some water. There, I'll feel better."

"Jackie, I hate to have to tell this to you . . ."

"What did Clifford do now?"

"I don't make it a habit to criticize other people's children . . ."

"Clifford has broken more people of that habit."

"Well, first . . . about the school books. The fifth grade hasn't any and Clifford volunteered to write his father to send some . . ."

Jackie laughed. "Smart, isn't he?"

"Yes, brilliant . . . but could you get him to write? Would his father send some books?"

"Oh, the kid's smart. His father's hunting. In Africa."

"I see. Well, we'll have to get some books some other way. The second thing. He tried to rent Gordy some filthy pictures . . ."

"Why, the little . . ."

Jackie stamped furiously out of the bedroom, shouting for Clifford. He was still on the balcony, hanging from the rail with one hand. I almost screamed when I saw him. If he fell . . .

"Clifford, you're still renting those pictures!"

"What pictures?"

"You know! At least I expect you to be honest!"

"What do you mean?"

"You know! Stop swinging and listen to me! You're cheating people. Those pictures aren't the least bit filthy. They're just photographs of some Rubens nudes. You got them at the Prado. Can't you see that's dishonest, Clifford? When people rent filthy pictures from you in good faith and then find out they're phoney, they're going to lose their respect for you, Clifford."

"Jackie," I said, "make him come in. Clifford, please come in on the balcony."

"Emmy, when I'm disciplining my child, I'll ask you not to . . . Clifford, I'm afraid I'm going to have to punish you."

"How? Look, left-handed!"

"No bullfight on Sunday."

"I hate bullfights!"

"Do you really hate them?"

"They stink."

"All right, then you have to go every Sunday for a month. Let's all go down to the beach, shall we?"

"Yeah," Clifford said. "I'm tired hanging around here."

He climbed back over the rail and we all took off for the beach. Clifford rented Gordy his skin-diving equipment and gave him instructions at a special rate. Jackie told me proudly that Clifford had almost three hundred dollars in a savings account in Switzerland and nearly five hundred invested in Germany. Krupp Steel.

"We're doing all right, aren't we?" Tom said, pulling on a sock.

"Hmm, dear?" I said from behind my lipstick.

"This party. Meeting all the writers so soon."

"Yes."

"It's really great to be part of something like this. Stimulating!"

"Yes."

"What a break, us meeting Jackie."

"Yes."

"Just think . . . we could be stuck over there in Torremolinos with a bunch of squares. These boys here, Jackie says, they're the real writers."

"Yes."

"They probably write all day and talk writing all night. Paris in the twenties. Hemingway and Gertrude Stein and . . . that crowd."

"Yes."

"What's wrong, Em? You're not very enthusiastic . . . you worried about something?"

"A little, yes."

"What?"

"Clifford is sitting with Gordy."

"Oh."

"Fifty pesetas an hour."

"It'll be all right," Tom said. "Tell Isobelita to lock her door."

The party was on the roof of a house just down the cliff from ours. Fortunately it was a flat roof as I was wearing high heels. I couldn't ever remember seeing so many bottles of liquor or so many plates of food gathered together in one place. Our host, Skip Cole, must have sold a seven-part serial to *The Saturday Evening Post*. Jackie introduced us to everyone, but as though no introductions were necessary. After it was all over I couldn't remember a single name, including my own.

Tom immediately found a man who, too, was writing his first novel. They gave each other the grip and went off, arm in arm, to a corner. I stood there alone, smiling. A triumphantly loaded young man weaved up to me and asked what I wanted to drink. Oh, anything, I told him, whatever you have the most of. He came back a moment later and handed me a glass of water.

"Thank you," I said. "You're so happy you must be Skip Cole. Congratulations on your sale."

He kissed me on the forehead. "What would you like to eat?"

"Oh, anything," I said, to see what would happen. "Whatever you have the most of."

He came back a moment later and stayed only long enough to hand me a large bowl of mayonnaise. Word must have got around quickly where the mayonnaise was. People kept walking by me, sticking things into it and thanking me. I listened to the fragments of conversation that jumped up out of the general buzz like popping corn.

". . . he writes too much! He's a windmill!"

"He made the eighteenth century for me . . ."

"Bookbinding is a lost art . . ."

"If I were Shakespeare, which of course I'm not . . ."

"I hate to tone it down, but Betsy threw up . . ."

"If I don't repeat myself, who will?"

"He had the nerve to offer me a five-thousand-dollar advance . . ."

"If he were my kid, I'd shoot him."

"I don't want the Nobel Prize!"

". . . but Conrad beat me to it. No, dear, not Nagel."

A blond, healthy woman dropped a lobster claw in my bowl (I still had the mayonnaise concession) and we got acquainted while she dug it out. It was I who broke the ice.

"Are you a writer?" I asked.

"No, honey," she said in the most charming Scandinavian accent. "I can't spell 'cat.'"

"Is your husband a writer?"

"Which one, honey?"

"Oh, you've been married more than once."

"Who hasn't? Oh, Cindy Ritt over there. I don't blame her, with her alimony. Three hundred American dollars a month. She lives like a queen. What is your alimony, honey?"

"I'm not divorced," I said self-consciously.

"No? A pretty girl like you! Well, don't worry, some day soon you'll find a husband."

"I have. I am married."

"How long?"

"Twelve years."

"Honey!" she said. "The alimony you will be able to get. You will live like a queen here. Good luck."

"I don't want a divorce," I said, feeling like a little girl. She shrugged. "It takes all kinds to make a world."

"There's no more mayonnaise," a man complained.

"Oh, sorry," I said. "Where's the kitchen?"

"I will get it," my Scandinavian friend said. "You go pick a fight with your husband." She took the bowl and went away.

The man stood there, looking at his piece of cauliflower.

"What are you writing?" I asked.

"Nothing," he said in overprecise English. "Absolutely nothing."

"You're not a writer?" I said, puzzled. "Do you get alimony?"

"Of course I am a writer, but I have not written a word for the past nine years. I will not write a word until the swine apologizes."

"What swine?"

"A certain critic whose name will not cross my lips until he apologizes."

"An American critic?"

"A German who writes for the Bad Liebenstien-Schwenin newspaper weekly."

"I've never been there," I said. "What did the critic say?"

"He misspelled my name. Unforgivable."

"I'm afraid I didn't . . . what is your name?"

"Banquert! The same as his!"

Herr Banquert stomped away. The kind Scandinavian brought me back the mayonnaise bowl all filled. She gave it to me, brushed aside my thanks, told me not to drop it, and drifted away. I was tired of mayonnaise; I found a table to put it on. Then I found a bench in a corner.

"The last well-bound book I read . . ."

"Sinclair Lewis, Somerset Maugham, James Branch Cabell and me . . . Herb Moody? I hope you're right, Jackie . . .

"She kept saying things like 'Nobody asked you to be a writer' and he finally said, 'What kind of an analyst are you anyway . . .'"

"It's the truth, he had the nerve to offer me a fifteen-thousand-dollar advance . . ."

"She shouldn't ever wear slacks."

"You think just plain Tom Wade is best . . ."

I became conscious of a figure at the other end of my bench, leaning back against the chimney. Whatever little it was wearing was black. All that I could see was a very oval white face, long white arms, and long white legs. The inertness of this being made me a little uneasy. I was wondering whether I should call the police or a priest when it spoke. Its voice was a moan with a British accent. It was directed at me.

"Never, never will I speak to one again."

"One what?" I asked, of course.

"God's vilest creature, a man."

"Oh, now, they aren't all that bad."

"You being an American can hardly know. When it comes to hurting a woman, American men are boys."

"We're a young nation," I said indignantly.

"I have been hurt by the English, the French, the Swedes, the Spanish, the Greeks, and one Dane."

"You should thank God," I said, "for the Iron Curtain."

"Most recently, by an Englishman again. That house up there." She unfolded one long arm and extended it toward our house; for a moment I thought she might touch it. "I can't bear the sight of it. I may burn it down."

"Oh, no, Adele! Could I get you some champagne?"

She lifted a bottle up out of the darkness to her lips. She drained it and threw it at the nearest man. He caught it and I noticed that none of the men had their backs turned to Adele.

"I was a Bluebell girl," she said, not to me or anyone particularly. "When I was fifteen I went to Miss Bluebell and said make me a Bluebell girl, I'm too tall for ballet and I must get away. My mother's lodgers are beginning to paw me. Miss Bluebell was a dear and I've danced at the Lido, in Paris of course, and in Vichy, in Glasgow, Madrid, Las Vegas, Reno, the Lido, in Paris of course, and Glasgow, Las Vegas, Reno . . ."

"Tolstoi had Russia, Balzac France, Joyce Ireland, I'm from New Rochelle . . ."

"Interesting, yes, exciting even, but abominably bound . . ."

"I'm another Falkner, Jackie, Scott Fitzgerald and O'Hara?"

". . . the nerve to offer me thirty thousand dollars . . ."

"I married when I was eighteen, but a Bluebell girl never breaks her contract . . ."

". . . wouldn't let Kazan or Logan touch it . . ."

"Emmy, I'm Sara Wicks. My husband is writing his first novel, too."

"Oh, hello. Our boys have got together. Has yours ever written anything before?"

"A little for the little magazines. They used his stuff for fillers."

"That didn't keep him busy."

"Oh, yes! He did his own typing and finally the pressure was too much, so we came to Monterojo where you can live for next to nothing and he could write his novel . . . oh, Cledge, this is Emmy Wade. Cledge writes for *Collier's*."

"*Collier's!*" I said.

Cledge nodded. "Sent a piece to them just last week. Fact is, they have several pieces of mine. Been holding them for some time now."

"*Collier's*," I said. "Do you do much for *Liberty?*"

"No, I'm strictly *Collier's* and always will be. I'm a loyal sort, pride myself on it."

". . . and there I was back in Reno again, but I wasn't a Bluebell girl anymore . . ."

"This is quite a party," I said. "That must have been quite a sale our host made."

"Best Skip has had in years," Cledge said.

"What was it exactly?"

"A yarn for *Tonight's Man.*"

"*Tonight's Man* . . . I don't think I've ever heard of it, but they certainly seem to pay well."

"Above average, actually. Two cents a word. Skip's check came to eighty-eight dollars and sixteen cents and he damned well needed it, too. Wife's having a baby, you know."

". . . but that isn't true, once a Bluebell girl, always a Bluebell girl . . ."

Suddenly it started to rain, a drenching downpour. Everybody except Adele made a grab for a bottle or a plate and headed for the stairs. Then somebody said, "Hey, it isn't raining anywhere else!" And another voice said, "It's only raining here!"

Jackie lifted her face up into the deluge toward our house.

"Clifford!" she hollered. "Drop that hose!"

Chapter Eighteen

"Now let's stay calm," I said.

It was a beautiful morning, bright but cool. The sun slanting in from over toward Egypt and the wind breezing down from the snow mountains did a delightful duet on our balcony. The sun, Juliet? The wind, Romeo? Yes. Birds sang, bells rang, flowers bloomed. Sky smiled, sea shone, sand sat. It was a beautiful, beautiful morning and it was ours.

Tom made an ecstatic noise.

Gordy said, "Wow!"

"What a morning," Tom said, "to start . . ."

"Now, now," I said, "that's exactly what I mean. Let's not get hysterical the way we did at home. No oohs, no ahs, no wild cheering. Let's not burn ourselves out beforehand. Let's just sit quietly down and start our book."

"All of us?" Gordy asked.

"Hush," I said, for the first time in my life.

"Yes, son, hush," Tom said. "Your mother's right. Let's not say what we're going to do. Rather let's say, this evening, what we've done."

"Yes, father. Hush."

Isobelita came hurtling wholeheartedly out onto the balcony, a vase of roses in her hands, a roof-raising smile on her lips. When she sensed our reverent mood, she lowered her high spirits like a sailor a sail. She tiptoed to the table and solemnly placed the roses on it amid the paper, the pencils, the dictionary, Roget's Thesaurus, Bartlett's Familiar Quotations. She turned to Tom, curtsied, her head bowed.

"Thank you," Tom said gruffly. *"Muchas gracias."*

"De nada," she whispered.

She smiled sadly at Tom, at Gordy, at me. She slipped away.

"She probably thinks," Tom said, "I'm going to do a new translation of the Bible or . . ."

"Hush," Gordy said.

He went to his father, shook hands, looking earnestly up into his face. Then, without a word, he walked quickly into the living room. I kissed Tom, holding his face for a moment in my hands. I went quickly into the living room to Gordy.

"Mother," he said with muted dignity, "it's time you accompanied me to school."

"True," I said. "Shall we proceed?"

I peeked back at Tom. He looked scared, absolutely petrified. He turned slowly to his desk, lowered himself into his chair. One hand pulled a pad of paper to him, his other reached across the brandy glass full of pencils and picked up another pad of paper. One hand didn't know what the other hand was doing.

The International School of Monterojo was up on the plateau of the village where the terrain took a well-deserved breather before it started climbing again. We opened an iron gate burdened by a heavy coat of arms and walked into a walled garden that was no longer very well cared for. It was a mess, a downright mess of magnificent flowers and blooming shrubs. The schoolhouse was a slightly dilapidated mansion that was a three-story ceramic. It was gingerbread, not in wood, but in tile of all the colors tile comes in. There were fancy tile chimneys, elaborate tile cupolas, extravagant tile balustrades. All the flat places were covered in tile murals. It looked like a Turkish bath turned inside out. I liked it. Gordy, on his first day at a new school, was too nervous to notice it. He asked me what was I looking at, Mom.

Classes had already started. Several small groups of little children and a teacher were scattered about the garden. We crossed a patio where a girl, wearing shorts and a halter and looking not much older than her pupils, was pointing at flowers.

"*La plumbagino*," the teacher said.

"*La plumbagino*," the children said.

"*La gardinia.*"

"*La gardinia.*"

"*La rosa . . .*"

We skirted the edge of a courtyard where an incredibly ancient olive tree sheltered a well and perhaps the third grade.

"Norway," a fat little fellow said with intense concentration, "Sweden, Finland, Denmark . . ."

We walked up wide stone steps, across a deep terrace and into a dark hall. "*Donde está Senora Wetzel, por favor?*" I asked. I asked it of a sturdy Andalusian lass scrubbing a fireplace of tile. She looked at me as if she had never heard anyone speak Spanish before. I repeated my question while Gordy cringed in embarrassment and pretended he wasn't with me.

"In here," a voice boomed.

The principal of Gordy's new school was seated in front of a tile coffee table, having coffee and croissants. She was a mammoth woman with a huge square face and strong arms. She looked like the guard who shaves off the girls' hair in women's prisons. I introduced myself, mentioning Jackie's name. Her mouth full, she nodded and patted the settee on each side of her. Gordy sat on her right, I on her left. She buttered a hunk of croissant, put marmalade all over it and handed it to Gordy without looking at him. He took it in surprise.

"You're American," she said to me. "Your husband with you?"

"Yes, he came over here to write a book."

"I had it in my mind to write a book over here. Warden

Lawes did a lot of good with his books. But I got involved in this school deal and . . ."

She shrugged, the settee shook. She gave Gordy some more to eat.

"Were you," I said, slightly confused, "in education back home?"

"Not exactly, but somebody had to start a school around here. I know the value of an education. I never had much myself."

"Well . . . thank you for starting the school."

"I got restless, to tell the truth, and I was glad for something to do. You can't spend thirty years in harness and then retire just like that. I guess I just have to have some people to look after, see they toe the mark and stay in line. How many years has the kid done . . . I mean what grade is he in?"

"Fifth."

"We got a fifth grade here," she said, pleased. "We opened it for Clifford."

"Yes, I know . . . but I understand you haven't any books yet."

"They ought to be here any day now."

"If you're relying on Clifford and his father . . ."

"I'm on to that punk. I cabled the librarian at the house to send me some. She'll take care of it."

"The house?"

"Women's House of Detention. New York."

"The ladies' jail in the Village? Yes, I know it!"

"Worked my way up to Assistant Warden there."

"My husband and I had our first apartment just around the corner!"

"A nice neighborhood. The fifth grade is down at the end of the hall if you want to put the kid in it."

"What about tuition? Shall I pay it now?"

"No, the fifth grade is on the cuff until we get it organized. Wait, I'll go with you. I don't like how quiet it is down there." She took us out into the hall, closed the door after her. She laughed and opened it again. "I can't get out of the habit of closing doors."

We passed a dormer window, framed in tile, that overlooked the fifth-grade patio. I could see Clifford and his teacher, sitting at a table. Clifford's teacher, a strapping blonde of about twenty, was wearing a bathing suit, a rather skimpy one by academic standards. Assistant Warden Wetzel, Ret., explained.

"We found," she said, "that it improved Clifford's attendance."

We stopped at the door for a moment.

"Maine," Clifford was saying, "Vermont . . . Vermont . . . Vermont . . ."

"New . . ." the teacher prompted.

"New Hampshire . . . what dumb names, why didn't they number them?"

The teacher said, "That wouldn't help you, Clifford. You can't count up to fifty."

"Fifty! Fifty states! Since when?"

"Since Hawaii and Alaska, you dope."

"Who let them in? They're always making more work for you."

"Maine, Clifford, go on . . ."

"Maine, Vermont, New Hampshire, Hawaii, Alaska . . ."

"The New England states," the teacher said, raising a clenched fist.

"Knock off for a minute, dearie," the principal said, leading us into the patio. "I got a new kid for you."

"Hi, Gordy!" Clifford said.

"Oh, God," the teacher said, "are you two friends?"

It was not without some misgivings that I left Gordy there in the fifth grade of the International School, and the chances of starting an effective PTA in this community seemed remote. Well, at least Gordy wasn't the victim of that American education malady, overcrowding.

I went to the market (*el mercado*). I bought bread (*pan*), butter (*mantequilla*), oranges (*naranjas*), bananas (*bananos* . . . real easy), onions (*cebollas*), artichokes (*alcachofas*), carrots (*zanahorias*), beets (*remolachas* . . . that one threw me!). When I pointed at the beets and the market lady said it for me, I couldn't repeat it after her to save my life. You're supposed to trill the "r" and when she did it, it sounded fine, like a motorcycle doing a fast getaway. I never could trill an "r" and when I tried it nothing happened except my tongue came out.

I felt like a complete idiot. At home you didn't have to have any talent to feed your family. A complete idiot could do the family buying in a supermarket for years without tipping her hand.

"R-*r-remolachas,*" the Senora r-r-rumbled.

Again nothing came out out of my mouth except my tongue. A crowd of Spaniards gathered around me. They joined the senora in my instruction, and the air thundered with trilling. It sounded like James Dean and his leather-jacketed buddies taking off for Malibu. Finally, I did it.

"R-*r-remolachas!*" I yelled.

"*Olé, olé!*" the crowd roared.

"R-*r-remolachas!*" I yelled again.

"*Olé, olé!*"

"R-*r-remolachas!*"

"*Olé, olé!*"

"*Dos orejas para la senora,*" a man shouted, "*y una pata!*"

"*Que?*" I said.

He pointed to his two ears and one of his feet.

I dug him. "*El toro!*" I said. "*Muchas gracias!*"

The crowd cheered and laughed and clapped its hands.

The market lady let me have my *remolachas* free of charge. When I protested I thought she was going to kill me. I have never heard such vindictive graciousness. I hurried away with my load. Altogether I had spent about eighty cents. I couldn't have carried any more.

The balcony of our house was empty. Tom wasn't on it. Not even his desk was on it. Fearfully, I looked over the railing and down the cliff. Skip Cole took one hand off his head and waved weakly up at me. I went into the bedroom to look for Tom. He wasn't there, but I could hear his voice.

"That's one way of looking at it, Jackie."

"I don't want to make the same mistake my parents made with me," Jackie said. "You can be too strict. It gives a child inhibitions. For instance, my father kept hammering at me and my brother how wrong it was to drink. He said alcohol was the root of all evil, not money."

"What did your father do?" Tom asked.

"Vice president of the Bend Savings and Trust Company. Well, I listened to all this yakkety-yak against drinking until I was such a mixed-up kid I was afraid to stay out later than Dad would let me and I didn't take my first drink until I was going on eighteen. And it was the same with sex . . ."

I hurried down to the patio.

"Well," I said to Tom, "I see you've got company."

"*Buenos días,*" Jackie said.

"Good morning," I said. "Couldn't you work on the balcony, Tom?"

"It's too beautiful up there. I kept looking at the scenery. So I moved down here and Jackie dropped in."

"I dropped in to see you," Jackie said to me.

"All right, let's go up on the balcony, Jackie."

"No, stay here," Tom said. "I've been sitting at this desk so long that I'm . . . I'll take a walk. I need it."

I waited until Tom was out of sight.

"Jackie . . ." I said.

"Emmy!" Jackie said. "The most wonderful thing! Herb Moody . . ."

"Jackie, listen . . ."

"Until the party last night Herb didn't know I existed . . ."

"Jackie, wait! Listen to me! Are you listening?"

"Yes, what . . ."

"Tom came over here to write. He took Gordy out of school, upset everything, and dragged us thousands of miles across the ocean because he couldn't write at home . . ."

"That often happens, you ought to understand how that can happen . . ."

"I do understand. I'm glad we came over here. But Tom must write here. He's got to get started . . ."

"He will."

"He won't if you drop in mornings and . . ."

"Don't worry about that."

"He's got to be left alone."

"Of course."

"No interruptions."

"Right, Emmy."

"No distractions."

"And no distractions."

"He needs peace . . ."

"Peace," Jackie said, "and quiet. Emmy, there are two beds in Gordy's room. Could you take Clifford for a week?"

Chapter Nineteen

"You'll hit me," I said.

"Have I ever hit you? Tom asked, but without indignation.

"You should hit me. How could I ever have done such a thing!"

"For God's sake, what did you do?"

"Put your arm around me."

"Sure."

"Say you love me."

"I love you."

"Emmy."

"Emmy, darling. Now what in God's name . . ."

"Remember the time when Gordy was a baby and he was teething and I was up with him all night, night after night after night . . ."

"Yes," Tom said impatiently.

"And we couldn't afford a maid so I had all the housework to do all day, besides taking care of Gordy, and the marketing and cooking . . . I was exhausted, almost dead . . ."

"Yes, yes . . ."

"And you brought Ollie Metcalf home to spend four or five days. Remember, dear?"

"Yeah, I remember, but what in the world . . ."

"How could you ever have done that to me, Tom?"

"Em, that was years ago!"

"But, Tom, tell me! How could you . . . whatever possessed you to do such a thing?"

"Well, I happened to run into Ollie . . . do you mean you've never forgiven me?"

"Oh, yes! Yes, yes, yes! I forgive you . . . no! No, there never was any forgiving to do! I never blamed you for a moment. But tell me, how was it you could do such a thing?"

"Well, it was Ollie's first couple of months in New York and he hadn't found a job yet. He was broke and lonely . . ."

"And you helped him!"

"Well, I . . ."

"Yes, you did! Don't deny it. He was your friend and he needed help and you helped him. I've always admired you for that, Tom."

"Oh, come on . . ."

"Yes, I have. You taught me a lesson I've not forgotten. To this day. Tom . . ."

"What!"

"Darling . . ."

"Oh, for God's sake!"

"Jackie is a much better friend of mine than Ollie ever was of yours."

"Okay."

"Now Jackie needs help. Tom, did you meet Herb Moody last night?"

"The little guy Jackie was buttering up?"

"Yes. Well, Herb wants to take her to Capri . . ."

"The Isle of Capri? You're kidding."

"They're crazy about each other."

"Well, what do we do? Lend them some money? I don't think that's a good idea."

"They have enough money. But you know that Jackie can't keep a maid . . ."

"Yeah, yeah. Come on, it's getting dark."

"Well, while Jackie's away . . . well, Clifford will be all alone, all by himself . . ."

"Why doesn't he come here and stay with us?"

"What!"

"There's an extra bed in Gordy's room."

"But your work! You couldn't write with Clifford in the house."

"Ernie Pyle used to write while the bombs were falling."

"Bombs, yes. But Clifford?"

"Well, for a couple of days."

"It's for a week."

"A week, Em?"

"Yes."

"He won't last a week."

"Who?"

"Herb Moody."

Clifford, of course, led the procession. He was carrying a trench coat, slung casually over his arm, a pair of binoculars in their case slung from one shoulder, a camera from the other. He was wearing a snap-brim hat, corduroy jacket, flannel slacks, and brogues. He also carried a tissue-paper-wrapped bottle and a copy of *Holiday* magazine. Behind him were five Spanish boys bearing his matched luggage. The tallest, a head shorter than Clifford, was toting the wardrobe-size case, the next a two-suiter, the next the one-suiter, the next the overnight bag, and the smallest boy was bearing a BB gun. They filed into the house, deposited Clifford's gear in Gordy's room, filed back out. Clifford, standing at the patio door, gave them each five pesetas as they walked by him. When they thanked him, they called him *senor*.

Clifford gave us his presents; the wrapped bottle to Tom, a tiny square box to me, and an envelope to Gordy. Tom opened his.

"Well!" he said. "Absinthe."

Quickly, I opened mine.

"Clifford!" I said. "An earring!"

"Only one?" Gordy asked.

"I gave the other one," Clifford explained, "to my Great Aunt Martha in Lake Forest, Illinois. I tried to buy only one, but my jeweler wouldn't break up the set. Aunt Martha only needs one."

"Why?" Gordy asked.

"She doesn't have any place to hang the other one. She . . ."

"All right, Clifford," I said. "Thank you for . . ."

"She lost one of her lobes you call them . . ."

"Yes, Clifford."

"Breaking up a dogfight."

"Open your present, Gordy!" Tom said.

Gordy did; I held my breath.

"Well!" Gordy said. "A check!"

"Why, Clifford!" I said. "How nice!"

"Just what I needed," Gordy said, and read his present aloud. "The Cook County Trust Company . . . pay to the order of Gordon Wade . . . two dollars . . . two and no one hundred dollars . . . C. A. Lynch. Thanks, Clifford."

"Would you mind," C. A. said, "not putting that through until after the first of the month?"

"Okay."

"It's time," I said, "for you boys to be off to school. Are you going to change your clothes, Clifford? Slip into a cap and gown maybe?"

"There isn't any school today."

"There isn't!" Gordy said.

"There isn't?" Tom and I said.

"No," Clifford said. "Spring vacation."

"The boys and I," I said to Tom, "will go to the beach."

"It looks like rain," Clifford said.

It rained for three days and three nights. Clifford taught us a strange new card game at which he was very good. He cleaned us out of pesetas and then won back Tom's absinthe, my earring, and Gordy's check.

"Darling," I said to Tom, "you could work. Gordy and I will play with Clifford. For matches."

"No," Tom said. "That kid's cheating and I'm going to keep playing until I find out how."

"We can't afford it."

"You and Gordy drop out. Listen, let's try moving the table over in front of that mirror, so I can watch Clifford from the rear, too . . ."

"I heard you," Clifford said from somewhere.

The sun, impatient to get back to Spain where it belonged, came out before it had completely stopped raining. There was a double rainbow. True, the second one didn't complete its arch; it was merely two spectacular columns sticking up out of the Mediterranean, but I felt justified in writing to Milly Talbot and Lois Baker that we had had two rainbows out front this morning at the same time. Milly would probably tell Bob that this was overdoing it, one rainbow at a time was enough for anybody. Lois probably wouldn't even mention it to Fred, but she would think it was cute of Spain.

Tom apparently couldn't wait to get to work. He shook the eucalyptus tree. By the time he changed his sopping clothes, the patio was ready for him, snug and dry. He sat down at his table, rubbing his hands enthusiastically. He even went so far as to pick up a pencil. Then he began to look over his shoulder, first one, then the other. Occasionally he would glance apprehensively up into the eucalyptus tree. He kept on doing this. I saw him mop his brow. I went to him.

"Darling," I said.

"Where is he?"

"Around someplace. He's being quiet."

"He's watching me."

"No . . ."

"I can feel him. Watching me, watching, watching . . ."

"Oh, Tom!"

"Clifford!" he shouted. "Clifford!"

There was no answer. The only sound was a damp euca-lyptus blossom landing on the table. The silence grew. I began to feel a little uneasy myself.

Tom said suddenly, "Why isn't Isobelita singing?"

"I've restricted her singing so you could work."

"Where's Gordy? Gordy!" Tom shouted. "Gordy!"

Gordy stuck his head out his bedroom window.

"What do you want, Pop?"

"Where's Clifford?"

"Right now I don't know."

"When did you see him last?"

"Little while ago."

"Where?"

"On the balcony."

"What was he doing?"

"Hanging by his feet."

"I'm going for a walk," Tom said.

"Mrs. Wade," Clifford said gravely.

"Yes?"

"Can I talk to you?"

"Of course."

Clifford sat down, crossed his legs, smoothed out his dress-ing gown, put his elbows on the arms of his chair and clasped his hands under his chin. "Mrs. Wade," he said again, and hesitated.

"Clifford," I said. "What is it? Do you miss your mother?"

"Who?"

"No, you were going to say . . ."

"I've been watching Mr. Wade."

"Oh. He thought so."

"Mr. Wade seems to be under some kind of strain."

"Well, now that you mention it . . ."

"If you were in Chicago, my psychologist is a very good

man . . . Mrs. Wade, tell me a little bit about Mr. Wade?"

"What, Clifford?"

"His background . . . stuff like that . . . you know."

"Really, I don't think . . ."

"Mr. Wade isn't functioning. He needs help."

"Clifford," I pleaded, "Clifford, don't you help him! Promise me that you won't help him . . ."

With horror I realized that Clifford had turned a deaf ear to me. The humanitarian smile on his face was macabre. "My Aunt Martha, the one that got in the dogfight," he murmured thoughtfully, "always says, all the time, misery loves company."

Chapter Twenty

Gordy and I were in the living room, wiling away the late afternoon with some Scrabble. Tom was out on the balcony, not in a good mood. He had spent several frustrating hours trying to find some barbed wire. He wanted to string it along the top of the balcony railing and possibly, he said, around his desk in the patio. I felt from the beginning that this was a waste of his time as Clifford undoubtedly had, somewhere in all that luggage, a pair of wire cutters from Abercrombie and Fitch, probably wrapped in the same oiled cloth as his mine detector.

"Is 'Q' always followed by a 'U'?" Gordy asked.

"I'm afraid so, dear."

Gordy groaned.

"I'm sure it feels much worse about it than you do."

Clifford strolled casually out of the boys' bedroom, a banana peel marking his place in *Fortune* magazine. He stopped at our table for a moment, so graciously that it raised my hackles, and gave us a little of his time. He made it clear that he endorsed family games, and more of them would make us a stronger nation.

"Go away," Gordy said. "Get lost."

"Don't be rude, dear," I said insincerely.

Unperturbed, Clifford examined the nails of his free hand. "You can't," he said, "get a good manicure in Spain."

He strolled out onto the balcony and sat in the chair nearest Tom. He smiled at Tom, who eyed him suspiciously. He opened *Fortune* at the banana peel, seemed to read. He kept nodding his head in approval and making small sounds of surprise. He underlined a lot with his Parker 88. Tom was

damned if he'd ask him what he was reading, but that took its
toll. Tom began to squirm in his chair and grip its arms.
Suddenly he said, "Where in God's name do you get all
these magazines?"
"I have a very good dentist," Clifford said.
Tom rubbed his forehead in silence.
Clifford said, "You seem jittery, Mr. Wade. Bad day?"
Tom grunted something that hardly answered Clifford's
question.
"Let's take a little walk, shall we, Mr. Wade?"
"No, let's not."
"Okay. We'll just talk."
"Let's just sit here. You finish underlining your magazine.
Why do you underline so much, Clifford, *what* do you under-
line, for God's sake?"
"Stuff I might want to read."
"You mean read again."
"No, read."
"You can tell," Tom said, his voice rising, "that it might
be interesting without reading it. That wasn't a question,
Clifford, don't answer it."
"What magazines do you read, Mr. Wade?"
"None. I have a lousy dentist."
"This book you're trying to write . . . is *it* going to be
funny, too?"
"Stop folding that banana peel, for God's sake! Put it
down somewhere. Clifford! I didn't mean down on the
beach!"
"What's your favorite fruit, Mr. Wade?"
"Well, Clifford, I'll tell you. I'm glad you asked me that
question. What was the question again?"
"Your favorite fruit. Don't tell me if you don't want to."
"I don't mind, Clifford. I'm not ashamed of it. Tomatoes.
Ha! I fooled you, didn't I? You thought tomatoes were a
vegetable."

"No, I knew," Clifford said calmly. "They used to be called love apples."

Tom rubbed his forehead. I could see Clifford surreptitiously making a note on a piece of paper he had clipped in his magazine. He looked thoughtfully at Tom for a moment or two.

"You like sports, Mr. Wade?"

"Yeah, yeah, yeah. Like sports."

"Did you play any sports in school? And if so, what?"

"Basketball mostly."

"Did you play for fun or to win? I mean, did winning mean a lot to you?"

"If the victory, Clifford, was well deserved, then only did I enjoy it. I never enjoyed winning merely for the sake of winning. Does that answer your question?"

"Just about," Clifford said, sneaking in a note. "We'll come back to that later. When did you first get interested in girls?"

"I've always been interested in girls. To the exclusion, in fact, of almost everything else."

"Do you remember your first girl?"

"Yeah . . . what was her name? Sally something . . . Sally Frew . . . Sally Frew!" Tom laughed and shook his head. "I haven't thought of her for years. Little Sally Frew, she lived way down Brighton Road and we'd read old comics together. Not books. Sunday comics. She had stacks of them. Oh, Lord, Sally Frew . . . I remember a new girl came to school and I thought she was pretty darn sweet and I was talking to her once and Sally hit me on the head with an apple core . . . Clifford, I guess you could sort of call that a love apple, couldn't you . . ."

"That'll be all, Mr. Wade."

"What?"

"That'll be all for today."

Clifford got up, walked in from the balcony and on to his room. Tom rose, looked after him, then slowly turned and stared out over the Mediterranean.

The next morning when I left for the market, Clifford was loitering in front of our house. He kept darting anxious glances up the lane and checking the hour on his Rolex. He saw me; he became chillingly nonchalant. He wet a finger, held it up into the breeze and murmured something about it being a great day to fly kites but a bad one to fight bulls.

I hurried through my marketing.

When I got back, out of breath, I found Clifford on the balcony, ostensibly working on his tan. He pretended to be dozing, but there was a very, very satisfied look on his face.

I went to our bedroom window to check on Tom. He was at his desk in the patio. His feet were up on it, alongside the feet of Cledge, the ball of fire who was still writing for *Collier's*. They were drinking coffee, smoking cigarettes, and talking their fool heads off.

That afternoon and evening Tom was in a much better mood; he was relaxed, enthusiastic, and confident. When Clifford joined him on the balcony, Tom looked at him as though he were a human being. They discussed vintage years for a few minutes, then Clifford slipped his pen out of his pocket and pretended to be doodling on the margins of the *Wall Street Journal* on his lap.

"Mr. Wade," he said, "were you an only child?"

Tom smiled and I could see that he was going to play along with Clifford; he said that he was an only child and waited politely for Clifford's next question.

"Which did you resent most? Your mother or your father?"

"I didn't have a favorite," Tom said. "I resented them equally."

"How did this resentment manifest itself?"

"I was sulky, uncommunicative. When I did speak, I always made sure my mouth was full. I'd wait to see which chair my mother or father wanted, then I'd sit in it real quick. I'd hide under beds and in closets until they called the police. When my mother made me take a bath I'd stay in the

tub until she came to see if I was all right, then I'd pretend
I was drowned."

"Say, that's a good one!" Clifford made a special note.
"Were you a good student?"

"Hell, no."

"Who was your father-image?"

"My father."

"I don't think that's allowed."

"I knew it wasn't. It was part of my rebellion."

"When did you first have this feeling of guilt?"

"What feeling of guilt?"

"That you have now."

"I don't have any feeling of guilt now."

"Have you always had it?"

"I never had it!"

"You felt inadequate and you tried to attract attention
by . . ."

"I've never felt inadequate . . ."

"You have this sense of failure . . ."

"What sense of failure!"

"That's all for today."

"Like hell it's all for today! Listen, you little . . . you go
to your room and you stay there until I tell you to come out!"

Skip, the *Tonight's Men* writer, and Leo, who was writing
his first novel, joined Cledge and Tom around Tom's desk
the next morning, and he was obviously delighted to have
them there. For quite a while I couldn't imagine what on
earth they were talking about.

"Great Length, Long Island," Cledge was saying as I tuned
in.

"Great Length?" Tom said. "You mean Great Neck?"

"Great Neck!" Cledge guffawed. "That's an odd name,
isn't it? You Americans. No, it was Great Length, not far
from Leave It Town . . ."

"Levittown," Skip said.

"Well, she was a lovely, lovely girl and I'm sure if I could ever get past my block I could do a lovely, lovely bit on her for *Collier's*."

"Can you finger the block?" Leo asked.

"Oh, definitely! My memory of her is so painfully poignant that I can't bear to think about her and really, you know, since the piece is to be about her . . . well, there you are."

"You just saw the girl twice?" Skip said.

"Just the twice."

"And you never spoke to her."

"Oh, yes. I spoke to her at Great Length."

Nobody said anything for some time. Isobelita served them coffee.

"Have you ever tried dictating it, Cledge?" Leo asked. "Sometimes you can talk things that won't seem to go down on paper."

"I've discovered, Leo, that you should never talk your stuff. A story told is a story never written."

They all thought about this for a spell.

"That's probably true," Skip said.

A few minutes later, Leo said, "Yeah."

After another long pause, Tom nodded.

They sat there. They crossed or recrossed their legs. They shouldn't have had that coffee. It was keeping them awake.

"I should never have accepted that advance," Leo said.

"How much was it?" Tom asked.

"Twenty-five hundred."

"Say, pretty good for a first novel. How long ago did you get it?"

"Two years this summer."

"Three years," Skip said.

"Three?"

"You've been in Spain three years."

"That's right. No wonder the dough's nearly all gone."

"Why," Tom asked, "do you think it was wrong to accept it?"

"It created a block. Instead of the novel being something I wanted to do, it became something I had to do. I find myself resenting this book, and until I get over this resentment I'm not going to start it. It wouldn't be fair to me or my publisher."

"Or your family," Cledge said.

"Or my family."

"What," Tom said anxiously, "does your wife think about it . . . it taking you so long to get started?"

"Toni's a great girl," Leo said. "In the last year or two she's been drinking too much, but she's a great girl."

"I don't remember," Tom said, "meeting her at the party."

"Thin," Cledge said, "grayish hair . . ."

I went to look at myself in the mirror.

"All her family," Leo said, "are prematurely gray."

"About time for a beer," Skip said.

"I'm sorry," Tom said, rising, "there's some wine around. I'm afraid that's all, but . . ."

"No, no, old chap! We have an iron rule. No alcohol in any form before eleven."

"I'm for that," Tom said.

"You'll come along then? The Bar Central?"

"Thanks, yes."

"Another twenty minutes," Skip said.

Tom sat down again.

Cledge said to him, "We were rather concerned about you at first. Madison Avenue, New York, all that. But you're fitting in. Yes! Welcome aboard."

"Listen," Tom said, "I didn't resign from one rat race to join another."

"Well said, old chap!"

"Wonderful thing about Spain down here," Leo said. "A writer can create his own tempo."

They all nodded.

"Create his own tempo," Leo said.

"Right," Cledge said, settling back in his seat.

"His own tempo," Skip said, not stifling a yawn.

"His own," Tom said, comparatively awake, "tempo."

Clifford scurried into the room and up to the window. He looked through it, beamed and nodded. "What's so good?" I asked him, remembering never to strike a child in anger who might strike back. Clifford pointed a finger at the patio.

"You know," Tom said, rousing himself, "people think Lincoln dashed off the Gettysburg Address in a few minutes on the back of an envelope, riding a train. No, that was merely a consummation. Actually, it took him all his life, more than fifty years . . ."

"See," Clifford said, "Mr. Wade is identifying. You've got to identify yourself with a group . . ."

"Yes, Clifford, thank you, thank you very much. Mr. Wade is now a member of the club."

"Jackie!" I cried, throwing my arms around her wholeheartedly. "I'm glad to see you!"

"Emmy!" Jackie said. She looked around the place. "I don't see any damage. I meant to tell you before I left that I'd pay for any damage. I always do."

"How was Capri?"

"It's as good a place as any."

"Is it a romance, Jackie? Might you get married, you and Herb?"

"Me marry Herb?" Jackie was aghast. "He's a writer."

"Sorry. I forgot."

"Clifford didn't break anything? Not even any bones?"

"He's been much too busy . . ."

"Clifford! I saw you! Come in here!"

Clifford came almost into the room.

"Hello, dear," Jackie said.

"You back already?"

"Give Mother a kiss," Jackie said.

"What for?"

"Come here, goddammit, and give Mother a kiss!"

"First what did you bring me?"

"Nothing! You've got everything!"

"I want two of everything."

"Shut up and start packing. God, Emmy, it's good to be back."

Clifford was pretty busy packing for the next two or three hours, but he managed to find a moment to assure me that there was no reason for me to despair. He wasn't walking out on me. I shouldn't worry. He would be dropping in from time to time to check up on Mr. Wade. It was late in the afternoon when he and his bearers filed away. Exhausted, but gratefully feeling the peace and quiet descend on the Clifford-less house, I flopped down on my bed. I dozed off. But not for long. The voices in the living room awakened me.

"Fine, thank you."

"How's Gwen?" Gordy asked.

"Fine, fine."

"How's Sue?"

"Fine, fine, fine."

"How's Polly?" Gordy asked.

"Fine," Bob Talbot said, "fine, fine, fine."

Chapter Twenty-one

"Milly and the girls," I said, "you couldn't bring them with you?"

"No," Bob said and chuckled. "No, I'm traveling light this trip. Well, Emmy! What a wonderful sunburn you've got! You and Gordy! Oh, it's good to see you, good!"

"It's good to see you, Bob. How long can you stay? How did you find us? What are you doing over here?"

Bob held up his hand, whispered. "Who's that? Tom?"

"Daddy," Gordy called. "Is that you?"

"Yeah. Me."

"Listen," Bob whispered quickly, "we'll have some fun. I'll hide out on that balcony. You make him guess who's here."

"Okay!" Gordy said. "Hurry, Mr. Talbot!"

Bob just got out of sight before Tom came into the living room.

"Darling!" I said.

"What's wrong?"

"There's somebody here and . . ."

"Oh, Lord! The minute we get rid of Clifford . . ."

"No, no!" I said hastily. "This is somebody you want to see!"

"I don't want to see anybody."

"Tom . . . this person is out on the balcony and . . ."

"What the hell are they doing out on the balcony, why don't they . . ."

"Tom, guess who it is!"

"I'm supposed to guess who it is?" Tom said, not looking forward to it at all.

"Yes. Think of the person you'd least expect to see here, but," I added hurriedly, "but one of the people you'd most like to see."

Tom just stood there. An awful silence fell on the Iberian peninsula. The birds, the bells, the burros, there was not a chirp, a clang, a bray among them. Finally Tom said, "Somebody I'd like most to see?" as if this were the stone to be left unturned to end all stones. If I had been Bob Talbot I would, as inconspicuously as possible, have hurled myself off that balcony.

Desperately, I mouthed Bob's name. Tom, bless him, merely looked at me as though I suddenly needed a doctor which, actually, I did. I tried spelling his name with my fingers but they shook so much that what I probably spelled was disaster. I ran around the room in small circles looking for a pencil and a piece of paper. All I got was dizzy. By now Bob must have thought we had left Spain. At last, throwing precaution to the wind, I went to Tom's ear and whispered into it. I had to do it three times. The third time I was sure Milly could hear me in Connecticut if she were near an open window.

"Bob Talbot?" Tom said, in not really the right way.

Bob came sprinting into the room. For a moment I thought he was going to keep right on going, but he stopped at Tom and pounded him above the elbows.

"Tom!" he shouted. "Tom, boy!"

"Bob."

"Tom! Tom, boy!"

"Well, Bob . . . well, you're the person I'd least expect to see here, but one of the people I'd like most to see. Emmy, look, hey, Gordy, it's Bob Talbot!"

"Where?" I asked. "Let's all sit down," I suggested.

"Bob," Tom said, "what are you doing here?"

When somebody asks you that question in that tone, you usually say, indignantly, that you have as much right to be here as they do, but Bob wasn't quite finished with the amenities. He said, "Tom, boy!"

"How did you find us?" Tom asked, as though Bob had used foul means.

"I couldn't locate you in Torremolinos, so I went to the American Express in Málaga. Tom, you look great!"

"How long can you stay?" Tom asked anxiously. "Are Milly and the girls with you?" he asked incredulously.

"No," I said. "Let's sit down!"

"Yeah," Tom said. "Yeah, Bob, since you're here you might as well sit down."

"Bob, dear," I said, "tell us everything. You came alone. It's a business trip. How are things on Madison Avenue?"

"Tom!" Bob said. "Rowe and Cohn lost the Artol account!"

"You're kidding, that could never happen!"

"It happened."

"What's with Lonnie Perkins now?"

"Went with Banning."

"Banning! No!"

"Chief copywriter," Bob said, nailing it down.

"So what's with Syd Drake, for God's sake?"

"Went with Kent, Buhl."

"Kent, Buhl!" Tom refused absolutely to believe that one. "No!"

"Took a cut."

"Who's out at Kent, Buhl? Anybody?"

"Kip."

"Not little Kippy!"

"He lost the key to the boss's heart. Buhl's daughter divorced him. Tom, it's been quite a spring on the Avenue! Quite a spring!"

"What kind of a spring," I asked, trying to sound casual, "has it been in our part of Connecticut? Wet? Miserable? We're lucky to be here?"

"Emmy, this spring has been fantastic! Gorgeous! Your wisteria and flowering quince, incredibly beautiful!"

"What about my jonquils?"

"Outdid themselves! Milly and I walked down our lane last Sunday to look at your place. Milly almost cried that you weren't there to see it."

"Say," Tom said, "Harley Nicholson should have been able to rent the house without any trouble. Do you know, Bob? Any news on that?"

Bob hesitated. "Gordy, would you get me a glass of water?"

"Yes, sir." Gordy got up off the floor. "Mr. Talbot?"

"Yes, son?"

"On Sunday did you notice about the air in my bike tires? In the garage?"

"Bike tires," Bob said blankly, then he came through. "Gordy, they're solid as a rock, ready to ride."

"They are! Gee, thanks for checking, Mr. Talbot."

When Gordy was out of hearing, Bob leaned across his lap toward us. He muted, solemnized his voice. "Emmy . . ."

"Yes, Bob?"

"Tom . . ."

"Yes, Bob?"

"Emmy, Tom . . ."

"Yes, Bob?" we said.

"Harley Nicholson hasn't got your house up for rental. He's trying to sell it. Does he know something about you two that Milly and I don't? No, I can't believe that. You are getting along now, aren't you? If you weren't, surely Milly and I would be the first to know. You would come to us, to Milly and me. We've always been . . ."

"Bob, wait!" Tom said. "Have you ever seen a happier couple?"

"On the surface, no. But underneath those tans of yours . . ."

"Bob," Tom said, "I'll slit Harley's throat on sight."

"Well, it's certainly been disturbing to your friends. Harley's almost never been wrong about marriages breaking up. He's often sensed it before either of the couple."

"That crumb," Tom said. "What about Ellie and Max Kinder? He's had their marriage a bust for years. Straight through three pregnancies . . ."

"Tom," Bob said, "Ellie filed last week . . . oh, thanks, Gordy."

"I hope you like it," Gordy said.

"Very good! A-a-ah, that hits the spot!"

"Bob," I said, "tell us about yourself. Have you run out of accounts to steal over there?"

"Emmy, Tom . . . I'm not here on business. No. Now I haven't told Milly any of this and I trust you not to mention it in your letters. Milly thinks I'm on a business trip, an extended business trip. But no. I'm on a six months' leave of absence from the shop . . . and it could become permanent."

"Bob," Tom asked anxiously, "what is it? The jitters?"

"The jitters?"

"Is it an ulcer, Bob? Lord, you, after all these years."

"No, not an ulcer. I've never felt better."

"Office politics, Bob? They're pushing you around . . . up and out, the old up and out, huh?"

"No . . ."

"Bob, I understand the Avenue. You can tell me the truth."

"Tom, it isn't anything that has happened. It's something that's going to happen, something big! You'll agree to that, I'm sure."

"Well, you've always been interested in government and you're a Harvard man . . . Bob are you going to be our next Ambassador to Spain?"

"Thanks, but no," Bob laughed. "Guess again!"

"I can't, I can't imagine . . ."

"Mind you now, not a word to Milly yet. I'm going to write a book."

"You," Tom said, "are going to write a book?"

"I came over here to write a novel."

"A novel?" Tom said.

"Boy!" Gordy said. "Are you lucky!"

"I won't tell Milly," I said.

Within an hour we had found Bob an apartment on the top floor of the house above us. If he dropped his watch out his living room window it would land in our patio. He moved a table over to the window, put his sparkling new typewriter on it. He unpacked a ream of yellow second sheets, two reams of white, and a sheaf of fifty carbons.

"There!" he said. "I'm all set!"

"You might find," Tom said, "that this room isn't the right spot for you to work in. You know, it's funny, but . . ."

"No, no, this'll be great!"

"You can't tell yet, Bob. Environment is a tricky thing, but don't get discouraged if you can't write here . . ."

"I'll write here! I can't wait to get started!"

I groaned for Milly.

"What name are you going to use to write under, Bob?" Tom said. "You know . . ."

"Robert Talbot."

"No, think about it, you better think about it, it's damned important. Will it make a movie?"

"A beautiful movie."

"Who should direct it?"

"Frank Capra."

"Bob, you can't make snap decisions like that. These things require thought and discussion. A director and casting can make or break . . ."

"Casting? Tony Perkins. Audrey Hepburn."

"Slow down! My God! Take it easy, kid . . ."

"Bob," I said, "you'll have dinner with us, of course. Isobelita is a wonderful cook. We'll have cocktails about seven and . . ."

"I'm not sure, Emmy. I thought I'd have a beer maybe, then a very light supper. I want to get up at seven, take a brisk walk and be at my desk at eight . . ."

"Bob," Tom said, "don't make unreasonable demands on yourself that will come back to torture you. The wonderful thing about Spain is that a writer can create his own tempo . . ."

I crept away to weep for Milly and the girls.

Cledge, Skip, Leo, and Tom sat around Tom's desk in our patio. They were silent. It was the silence of the appalled. From time to time they would lift their heads, sometimes individually, sometimes in gruesome harmony, to look up at Bob Talbot, splendidly, indeed majestically, framed in his window. Bob was completely unaware of them.

"He started at eight?" Cledge asked hoarsely.

"On the dot," Tom said.

"Look at him," Skip said.

"He never gets off that chair," Leo said.

"He doesn't smoke."

"He never makes a mistake."

"He doesn't ever stop to think."

"He writes and writes and writes."

"Is that an electric typewriter?" Skip asked.

"No," Tom said.

"Look at him."

"It can't be any good."

"It's got to be drivel."

"There . . . he's stopping . . ."

"No, a new sheet of paper."

"Look at him."

"He's smiling."

"He enjoys it."

"Who does he think he is!"

"Coming in here like this!"

"The sonuva . . ."

"Take it easy, Skip."

"Put down that rock."

"Well," Cledge said, "Monterojo was a beautiful place."

"It was too good," Leo said, "to last."

"There are still a few villages up the coast toward Alicante that haven't been discovered. Roads are damn near impassable."

"And there are a couple of Greek islands that are fairly inaccessible."

"Look at him."

"Tom, what are you going to do?"

Tom didn't seem to hear him.

"Well, so long, Tom."

"Good knowing you, Tom."

"See you sometime, Tom, I hope."

They went away.

Tom lifted his face toward Bob's window. He put his hands over his ears for a moment, then he rose and walked slowly around the eucalyptus tree. Suddenly, he strode to his desk. He took paper and pencils from its drawer, slammed them down, pulled up his chair and flung himself into it. The back of his neck bristled with determination. But the incessant clatter of Bob's typewriter was too much. He snatched up a pad and pencil and marched resolutely out of the patio to find a quiet place to work.

Chapter Twenty-two

"What's for lunch, Mom?"

"*Una tortilla y una salada.*"

"Not *salada, ensalada.* Say it three times."

"*Ensalada, ensalada, ensalada.*"

"Boy, would a hot dog taste good. I could even go for a TV dinner. You know, they weren't so bad."

"It was TV. How was school?"

"I liked it better before our books came. Did you have radio dinners when you were a little girl?"

"No. Are your hands clean?"

"This one is. This one isn't very. Where's Daddy?"

"Off someplace working."

"He got a job!"

"No, he's writing. It was too noisy around here. Mr. Talbot's typewriter."

"Yeah, you can hear it clear in here. He sure can type! Mr. Talbot walks fast, he talks fast, he types fast."

"He's fast. Wash your hands."

"Did you say Daddy was writing? Really writing, you mean?"

"I wouldn't be surprised."

"Clifford! He did it after all!"

"I think it was more Mr. Talbot who did it."

Isobelita bloomed into the doorway, breathlessly eager to announce her glorious news. The first few times she went through this I expected her to say at least that the English had given Gibraltar back to Spain. But now I knew better. Lunch.

"*Senora!*" she shouted, quivering with joy. "*Almuerzo!*"

"You'd think," Gordy said, "we were having hot dogs."

"*Gracias, Isobelita,*" I said. "*Nosotros vengemos.*"

"*Venemos,* Mom. Aren't we going to wait for Daddy?"

"I guess he'd rather write than eat."

"Hey!"

"*Senora, donde está el senor?*"

"*El Senor está . . . no sé exactemente.* What did I say, Gordy?"

"You don't know exactly. Very good, Mom."

"*Isobelita,*" I said proudly, for no wife had ever been so pleased to be able to say that she didn't know where her husband was, "*no sé exactemente donde está el senor. Muy bien?*"

"*Si, senora!*" Isobelita was twice as proud of me as I was. Her cyclonic laughter threatened the roof, making me wonder again how such a pretty girl could be so loud. "*Estupendo, senora, estupendo!*"

"What a day, what a day!"

"Congratulations," I said.

"What a start! Chapter one!"

"Why, you worked right through lunch."

"Fourteen pages!"

"Wonderful! You deserve a drink . . ."

"No, no, none of that, don't tempt me. Where's Tom?"

"I don't know, Bob, he's been gone since about ten this morning."

"You don't know where he went?"

"Off someplace to write . . . you know, the beach, up on the cliff . . ."

"Inspiring, yes! Say, it's almost six. The boy is having himself quite a day, too. By God, Emmy, this is terrific! The two of us here together, writing! We'll knock them dead! The Book-of-the-Month Club! Tom and me! The Dual Selection!"

"Gordy, eat your dinner."

"I'm not hungry."

"Darling, there's nothing to worry about."

"Then why aren't you eating your dinner?"

"Let's both eat. We're being silly."

Gordy picked up his fork, looked carefully through his *paella* and found the smallest piece of chicken. He divided it into three shreds, put the shortest in his mouth. I took a dwarf leaf from my artichoke, touched it to the mayonnaise, and nibbled off its end, nearly missing it completely. We sat in silence, gorging ourselves, listening for a footfall, a door opening, a cheery hello. We heard an airplane, a dog barking, Isobelita slap her.

"It's dark," Gordy said. "He couldn't still be up on the cliff or someplace writing in the dark. Where could he be?"

"Darling," I said, getting a grip on myself, "it really is silly to worry. If we had a telephone he would have called long ago to tell us where he is. He probably got offered a ride into Málaga and there was something he wanted to do . . . like buy you a present maybe, that snorkel . . . and the car broke down, something like that. He'll be popping in any minute now. No reason to worry. Da-da-de-da-da. Please pass the bread . . . the *pan* as we Spanish say . . . da-da-de-de-da-da . . ."

"Mom, why don't you go to bed?"

"Gordy! You get back in bed!"

"He's all right, Mom, stop worrying."

"Why, of course he's all right."

"Sure," Gordy said, putting a consoling hand on my arm. "He couldn't have fallen off that cliff."

"Of course not! That never occurred to me."

"Me neither. And besides some places it isn't very high. If anything had happened to him we would have heard from the hospital."

"Yes, dear."

"He probably just got . . . you know, delayed. He's probably helping somebody fix their lawn mower." Gordy whistled a few bars of "The Star Spangled Banner." "Remember when he fixed Mrs. Weller's lawn mower for her? It took him all day Saturday and Sunday. So he mightn't be back until tomorrow night." Gordy whistled quite a lot of "God Bless America." "And Mrs. Weller had to get a new lawn mower. You might as well stop smoking and walking around and go to bed, Mom." Gordy yawned like everything. "I am. Boy, am I sleepy! I'll probably be asleep before my head hits the pillow if I used a pillow. Good night, Mom." Gordy went back into his bedroom, whistling "My Country 'Tis of Thee."

"My second," Jackie said, "didn't come home once for five or six days. But I didn't sit around biting my nails."

"What did you do?"

"Met my third. And once that one was gone for two weeks. Not a word from the punk."

"Now that must have upset you a little, Jackie."

"Well, to tell you the truth, until almost the end of the first week I really didn't notice he wasn't around. By that time I was used to it and didn't mind."

"Where was he?"

"I never gave the crumb the satisfaction of asking. It drove him nuts. Don't you ask Tom. It'll kill him. Then my last one! He made me appreciate the others. I didn't know when I was well off. I always knew where that one was. Night after night after night he was right there in front of the television set."

"Jackie, listen!"

"Yes, there's someone . . ."

"Tom?" I called.

"Let me handle this," Jackie said. "You stay out of it."

"He's my husband."

"Only your first. Sit down."

"Oh, Bob," I said. "Hello."

"Hello," Bob said. "Tom back yet?"

"Not yet."

"I thought not. Emmy . . ."

"What is it, Bob, what's wrong?"

Bob was not himself. His face, despite being normally red, had somehow managed to become flushed. It was now a deep maroon. I had never seen a hair of his silver head out of place. Now a whole handful of it was unmoored. There was something generally unhinged about him.

"Bob! It's Tom, you . . ."

"Emmy, I know where Tom is."

"You've seen him?"

"No, but it's obvious where he is. Put yourself in his place. He had a great day. Picture it! It's thrilling. Today high up on a cliff overlooking the Mediterranean or somewhere down on its shore, Tom Wade realized himself. His dream came true. Tom became a writer. After all the years of frustration, his years in the Army, his years on the Avenue and lately the weeks of uncertainty as he took the plunge and momentarily floundered . . . after all that, today Tom finally made it. I know what he felt. The same thing happened to me today. I know what it means to Tom. I know what he did. Emmy, he celebrated his triumph. He had one drink, then another and another. That's where he is . . . going from bar to bar, getting gloriously loaded. I know that, I understand that . . ."

"But, Bob," I said, "you didn't get drunk . . ."

"Oh-oh," Jackie said.

"Bob!" I said.

"My Gawd," Jackie said, "he's passed out."

"Let's get him here on the sofa."

"Gawd, he's heavy. Emmy, if Tom isn't home by tomorrow morning, let me know. I'll take care of it."

"How? The police?"

"No. Clifford."

"Clifford will find Tom?"

"Just offer a reward."

Clifford surveyed us calmly. He settled down in his chair, crossed his legs, folded his arms over the Phi Beta Kappa key he wore to school and looked from me to his mother to Bob Talbot, whose normally red face was a bit faded this morning. Clifford cleared his throat. We all leaned forward. Clifford liked that. He cleared his throat again.

"Clifford," his mother said dangerously.

"Mother?" Clifford asked, equally dangerously.

"Please," I said.

"Mrs. Wade," Clifford said, "where's Gordy?"

"He went out to look," I said. "With Isobelita."

"That's good," Clifford said. "This is no place for children."

"Clifford," Jackie said, "if you found Mr. Wade, you tell us quick or I'll break . . ."

"Mrs. Wade," Clifford said, "about the reward."

"If you don't think it's enough," I said, "I'll make it ten dollars."

"Okay, but what I meant was . . . does it go for information leading to his whereabouts, too?"

"So you didn't find him," Jackie said.

"But I know where he went. How about it, Mrs. Wade?"

"The ten dollars is yours. Please, Clifford . . ."

"And expenses?"

"Yes!"

"All right." Clifford took a notebook from his pocket. "Now when you last saw Mr. Wade he was wearing a corduroy jacket, blue shirt open at the neck, pants, no socks and shoes. Right?"

"Yes, yes . . ."

"He was about six feet, a hundred and eighty when you last saw him, dark hair, brown eyes, no scars . . ."

Bob Talbot got up and took a step toward Clifford.

Jackie said, "If you touch that kid . . ."

"Please!" I said.

Bob sat down, groaning.

"A man," Clifford said, referring to his notes, "answering to that description was seen entering Pogo's Bar in Monterojo about five o'clock yesterday afternoon. He had two beers, then three brandies and soda. From there he went to the Bar Central and had one beer, then four brandies and soda. Then he bought champagne for everyone and they drank to . . . and I quote Mr. Wade . . . 'the greatest day of my life.'"

"Emmy!" Bob said. "I told you!"

"Then Mr. Wade," Clifford said, disapproving of Bob's interruption with a malignant glance, "made a speech. Mrs. Henry Falter-Woodling told me it was the finest barroom speech she ever heard and she said she wished that Falter-Woodling could have hung on another fifteen years to hear it, too. Mrs. Falter-Woodling remembered quite a lot of it." Clifford wet the tip of his index finger and flipped over a page of his notebook with practiced ease. "Again I quote. 'Yes, ladies and gentlemen, this is indeed the greatest day of my life. I have had my moment of truth.'" Clifford looked up. "Mrs. Falter-Woodling said he was standing on the bar by then and behind him there was a big bull fight poster and it was all absolutely incredibly top drawer. 'Moment of truth. I have found myself. I know I can't write.'"

"What!" Bob said. "Impossible!"

"Knows he *can't* write?" I said.

"Correct," Clifford said.

"Tom," I said. "Oh, Tom."

"He said it was a mistake to ever think he could and he should never have quit his job . . ."

"I don't believe it!" Bob said. "How reliable is this Mrs. Falter-Woodling?"

"She," Clifford said coldly, "is a distant relative of Winston Churchill."

"Sorry," Bob said.

"If I may continue . . . Mr. Wade said he finally realized that he never wanted to write. He just wanted to be a writer. Without the blood, sweat, and tears. That was when Mrs. Falter-Woodling told me she was a distant relative of Winston Churchill. Then Mr. Wade said . . . and Mrs. Falter-Woodling and I both agreed he put it rather well . . . that he wanted to enjoy the end without suffering the means."

"That is good," Bob said. "Of course he can write!"

"Then there was a long pause and then Mr. Wade raised his bottle and said, 'To Emmy and Gordy, to whom it shouldn't have happened and never will again.'"

"Oh, Tom," I said. "Tom, where are you?"

"Mrs. Falter-Woodling told me that people who couldn't even understand English were crying. Then he picked himself up, brushed himself off . . ."

"Picked himself up!" I said.

"Oh, sorry. First he fell off the bar, then he picked himself up and walked out of the bar without looking back. Mrs. Falter-Woodling said he was smiling the saddest smile she ever saw. That was about quarter to seven. There's only one more bar in Monterojo, the Spanish joint. I went there and asked if Mr. Wade had been there. *Un Americano,* I told them, *mucho drunko. Si,* they said, *mucho drunko,* and they described him to me. It was Mr. Talbot."

"Who?" Bob said.

"You," Clifford said.

"Have you any more information," Bob said, "about Mr. Wade?"

"Yes, I found a taxi guy that took him to the Málaga airport."

"Málaga airport," I said.

"I went to the airport . . . that's the expenses, Mrs. Wade."

"All right . . ."

"Mr. Wade tried to buy three tickets to New York . . ."

"Tom," I said, "Tom, Tom."

"But they wouldn't honor his credit card. Then he went into the airport bar and had some more to drink and bought drinks for everybody and then he bought a ticket to Tangier."

"Tangier!" I said.

"That's in Africa," Clifford said.

"It's only forty minutes by plane from Málaga," Jackie said.

"Did he get on the plane?" I asked Clifford.

"Yeah, he got on okay. Don't worry about that, Mrs. Wade, he didn't miss his plane. I found that out for sure."

"What's he doing in Tangier?" I wondered hysterically.

"He probably," Jackie said, "drank everything in southern Spain."

Chapter Twenty-three

"Take me," I said, without thinking it the least bit amusing, "to the Casbah."

The cabdriver, swarthy, shifty-eyed, broken-nosed, gold-toothed, shrugged his narrow, brutal shoulders. Obviously if I, a woman alone, unveiled, not unattractive if she could believe her mother, insisted upon going to the Casbah of the world's leading Sin City, it was no more his concern than if I never returned. He smiled a modest, sadistic smile as he knocked the ash from his pipe. Tobacco ash to the unsuspecting, but I knew better. Not tobacco, but *kef*, a marijuana substitute used as widely in Tangier as we use margarine instead of the seventy-cent spread. He meshed his gears.

We ricocheted up a wide street that looked, deceptively, like Euclid Avenue in Cleveland, Ohio, except for the sidewalk cafés that spilled out of the bottoms of most of the office buildings, what were apparently office buildings. We swung right and down a less wide street that looked, deceptively, like that street in Bridgeport, Connecticut where the Goodwill people have their place.

My eyes, forsaking for a moment their search for my husband, met the driver's in the rear-view mirror. He grinned gold at me and his right arm snaked over the back of his seat toward me. He was holding a picture up for me to see. I tried in all decency to avert my eyes, but it was too late. Amazed, I stared at the picture. It was a charming snapshot of three beautiful children between the ages of five and ten. They were angelic. The driver made a guttural sound that claimed them as his own.

I wasn't taken in for a second. Never had I encountered a more blatantly hypocritical bid for an overgenerous tip. Those three angels were no more his than mine. God knows how he got his treacherous hands on the picture. Probably stole it from some kidnaping crony who had a Polaroid. I clucked noncommittally at the snapshot and looked out the window for Tom. He was nowhere to be seen.

The cab swerved into a large plaza, passed a theater playing Walt Disney's *Bambi*, and drew up to the forbidding but, oddly enough, at the same time, beckoning gates of the Casbah. Briskly, hoping to make the driver think I knew the currency, I thrust a handful of dirhem at him. He counted them, smiled, and shook his head, the robber. I opened my purse, but again he smiled and shook his head, and handed me back one of the dirhem notes. Stunned, I thanked him and turned away. Only then did I realize the money he had refunded was, of course, counterfeit.

I plunged into the Casbah.

The sounds and smells of the narrow, crowded passages were overwhelming, an exotic, sinister tumult. Making myself as small, as unobtrusive as possible, I sidled through the robed mob, looking for a fellow in a corduroy jacket. The alleys were lined with hole-in-the-wall stalls selling, as I well knew, stolen goods, smuggled stuff, or at least merchandise so phony it wouldn't fool a child. Even the artificial fruit looked phony and I touched a grape to see if it wasn't really real. The few on-the-up-and-up appearing places were fronts for dens of heaven-knows-what.

I plunged deeper into the Casbah and the depravity became more open and above board. A juke box blared out the frenetic frustration of one of America's millionaire junior citizens. I hesitated at the intersection of two murderous-looking slits between the ancient buildings. A veiled young woman moved sinuously to my side. Her voluptuous brow, her world-weary eyes were all I could see of her face. What did she want of me? I could imagine. She wanted me to help her escape from this place. She wanted to lead a respectable life, to marry . . .

"May I help you?" she asked.

"You speak English!" I said.

"Oh, yes," said the voice behind the veil.

"Where did you learn?"

"Mount Holyoke. You seemed to need help. Are you lost?"

"Not exactly. Actually," I said, telling lies, not realizing that if I succeeded in pulling the wool over her eyes I wouldn't be able to see any of her face, "I'm to meet my husband here for a drink. Where is the biggest bar? The bar where a typical American would end up. You know what I mean," I added roguishly.

"All the bars are gone. You can't get a drink here anymore."

"You can't get a drink here! Not even a drink!"

"Just mint tea. And Coca-Cola."

"What a way," I said, "to run a Casbah."

"Call me Mohammed."

"Mohammed," I said, "whatever happened to the Casbah?"

"The end of the International regime, that did it. Tangier is no longer a free city. It is not like it was a few years ago. We are Moroccan now."

"But a man can still get a drink in Tangier, can't he?"

"Oh, yes. In the new town. The European sector."

"You have tourist traps, don't you?"

"*Mais oui!* We have splendid tourist traps."

"Take me to the best."

"A pleasure."

"It was nice of you to wait for me, Mohammed."

"An honor."

"What are your little girls' names?"

"Ava," Mohammed said, "Lana, and Liz."

There was no one remotely resembling my husband as I remembered him in the first tourist trap. Nor in the second, nor in the third. Mohammed and I ran out of tourist traps. We did the low-budget, crumby bars and finally, our backs to the wall, we desperately cased the respectable joints. We went up the rues de Bach, Beethoven, Mendelssohn, Chopin, and Wagner, a surprisingly quiet street. We went down the rues de Rembrandt, El Greco, Goya, and Velázquez. No luck. Then I wondered if Tom, bidding adieu to his dream, mightn't be wandering along the rues de Tolstoy, Cervantes, Molière or Victor Hugo. He wasn't. As I limped, empty-handed, out of Il Inferno on the Rue Dante, it occurred to me that Tom might be sleeping it off in some hotel by now. In fact, he'd better be.

I dragged myself across the lobby of still another hotel and hopelessly said for the seventh time to the seventh clerk, "Is there a Mr. Tom Wade registered here?"

"Yes," he said.

"Thank you," I said dully, tonelessly, and turned away. Then I turned back and asked, "What did you say?"

"There is a Mr. Tom Wade registered here."

"There is!"

"Yes, madame. Room twenty-eight."

"Twenty-eight . . . is he in his room now?"

"He isn't."

"He isn't?"

"But Mrs. Wade is," he said.

"Mrs. Wade is," I said.

He nodded.

"Did I understand you to say," I said, "that Mrs. Wade is upstairs in Mr. Wade's room?"

"Yes," he said.

"I see," I said.

I sat calmly in a corner of the lobby, smoking one cigarette after another. There was no call for hysteria. There was no reason to send a cable. An airmail letter would do nicely. "Dear Harley, sell the house immediately, find small apartment for Gordy and me . . . oh, Harley, Harley, Harley, how could he do such a thing? Sincerely, Mrs. Thomas Wade."

"Mrs. Thomas Wade!" a voice called. "Mrs. Thomas Wade!"

I dried my eyes, struggled to my feet, and headed across the lobby toward the boy soprano in the fez who was singing my name. A great blond creature with long green earrings and tight pink slacks got to him first.

"Mrs. Thomas Wade?" he asked her.

"That's right, Buster," she said.

"Telephone. This way, please."

She slunk after him, her pink slacks slinking after her. He held open the door of the phone booth for her. She patted him on the fez, filled the booth with herself, closed the door, and took the call. I edged closer to the booth. I couldn't hear a thing, but I could see that she was talking to someone who was a buddy of hers. It was a call she was glad to get; she couldn't have been more pleased.

"Mrs. Wade!"

"You mean me? Oh, hi, Mohammed."

"Mrs. Wade, I have news of your husband."

"I don't want to hear it."

"Truly?"

"Oh, well, since you've been so kind . . ."

"I have talked with the concierge. Your husband took the ferry to Algeciras this afternoon."

"You're certain it was my husband?"

"The concierge had to walk him around the Place de France six or seven times before he could sit upright in a taxi."

"That's my husband."

"The concierge is very fond of him. He has never known an American to be so generous . . ."

"Oh, dear."

"Nor to look so well in a fez."

"Where is Algeciras?"

"Spain. Just opposite Gibraltar."

"Could you tell me," I said to the desk clerk of a hotel just opposite Gibraltar, "if a Mr. Thomas Wade is registered here?"

"No," he said coldly.

"Thank you," I said.

"But Mr. Wade has been here." He nodded grimly across the lobby. I turned and saw two workmen repotting plants. "I have clerked in hotels from Lisbon to Bangkok and I have never seen a man with such an aversion to potted plants."

"Was he wearing a fez?"

"Yes. On top of a turban."

"So Mr. Wade was here, but he didn't register."

"Exactly. Couldn't hold a pen."

"Where is he now?"

"God knows. But you might ask Mrs. Wade."

"Mrs.," I said, able to speak, "Wade?"

"She's in the bar."

My color returning, I said hopefully, "Mrs. Wade . . . she couldn't, by any chance, I suppose, be Mr. Wade's mother?"

"Decidedly not."

"Not old enough, I imagine, to be his mother?"

"No, she's his wife. Dreadful for her, of course."

"Young man," I said, getting back my perspective, "V. S. Pritchett wasn't kidding."

"I beg your pardon?"

"There are indeed vestiges of harem life in Andalusia. Where is the bar?"

"To the right."

"Thank you."

"If Mr. Wade should come in, God forbid, whom shall I say was inquiring for him?"

"Mrs. . . . just say Gordy's mother."

As I crept, inept, into the nearly empty bar, it didn't surprise me in the least to discover that the moment Tom's back was turned the local (Algeciras) Mrs. Wade was lowering her lashes at another man. A man whose facial thrust, due partly to an ill-advised attempt to hide a too-strong chin behind a goatee, was alarming. His forehead, though low, added to this situation by bulging. His trapped nose protruded desperately. I liked him instantly. This Mrs. Wade was just as spectacular as the Tangier Mrs. Wade. They both had the same bigness, blondness and overwhelming animal health, and it struck me how true it was that men so often leave one woman to take up with another very much like her. Tom was no exception.

I sat at a table close behind Mrs. Wade and her new playboy, hoping that if Tom happened to come in unexpectedly and find them together he wouldn't make too ghastly a scene. Obviously, Tom knew this place, and vice versa. Every other one of the long-stemmed bar stools had been bent until its seat touched the floor. They seemed to be bowing from the ankles. I ordered a vodka martini in my best Spanish and the waiter brought me a rum and Coca-Cola. I sipped it and listened.

"I'm not a boy," he said petulantly.

"Nowadays," she drawled, "fewer and fewer men are."

"I'm not getting any younger. I want to know where I stand. I have to think of my future. All my friends have been married at least once."

"Lay off it awhile, Buster. I'm nervous."

"About him?"

"I caught him drinking coffee. He was trying to sober up."

"Good Lord!"

"I got some cognac into his coffee in time. He had four more cups and the last one was straight cognac."

"Was that when he threw the potted plants?"

"No." She nodded at the bar stools. "That."

"Expensive, isn't he?"

"He's costing a fortune."

"Well, it takes money to make money and you can take him off your income tax."

"Funny, funny, funny."

"What if they get him? What will they do to him?"

"Oh, shut up, they won't hang him."

"There are worse things than hanging."

"Stop it, Buster!"

"I like him!"

"So do I!"

"I've noticed that."

"Stop it, he's a happily married man. Emmy, Emmy, Emmy, if I ever hear that name again!"

"Who's this Gordy?"

"His kid."

"His kid! I thought he was at least president of Standard Oil. Who's Bob Talbot?"

"I couldn't figure that out. Shall we have another drink?"

"Not for me," he said.

"I shouldn't either," she said. "I should stay sober."

She drummed on the table with her long, blood-red nails and hummed "Stardust." He joined in. They obviously had done a lot of humming together.

"I love you," he said fiercely.

"You're hurting me," she said. Then, overcasually, she said, "Are you wearing your contact lenses?"

"Just one of them," he said petulantly.

"Where's the other one?"

"I don't know and I don't give a hoot."

"I know and I give a hoot. You should be more careful. Here."

"Thanks. Where did you find it?"

"The maid found it under my bed and it was damn embarrassing." She looked at her watch. "Unless the boat's late, he should be there by now."

"Where?" I said.

"Tangier, you dope," she said.

"I didn't ask you," he said.

If they looked over their shoulders, I was gone. I stopped long enough in the lobby to give each of the two workmen who were finishing up the potted plants fifty pesetas. They were bewildered but grateful.

Chapter Twenty-four

"Are your blindfolds all in place, panel?" John said. "Yes," panel said. "All right, Mystery Challenger," John said, "come in and sign in, please!"

There was a mere sprinkling of applause, then the squeak of chalk on blackboard. "Sets the teeth on edge, doesn't it?" I whispered to Arlene. She whispered back, "I'm used to it."

"We'll begin the questioning," John said, "with Arlene."

"By the lack of applause," Arlene said, "I gather you are not in show business."

The Mystery Guest, in a thick Italian accent, said that Arlene was right.

"Bennett," John said.

"Are you a man?" Bennett asked.

The Mystery Guest, in a thick German accent, said that Bennett was right.

"Dorothy," John said.

"Did you and I have dinner at the Pavillon last week?" Dorothy asked.

The Mystery Guest, in a thick French accent, said no, they did not.

"Emmy," John said.

"Are you," I asked, "Thomas Wade?"

"Yes," Tom said.

I tore off my mask, started to my feet, my arms outstretched. The Mystery Guest's chair was empty. Tom was gone.

"Good night, Emmy," Arlene said. "Good night, Dorothy," I said. "Good night, Bennett," Dorothy said. "Good night, John, leading and beloved news analyst and moderator," Bennett said. "Good night, Bennett," John said, "and good luck on your lecture tour. Where are you off to this time?"

"Tangier," Bennett said, "and Algeciras . . ."

I awoke and sat up, rubbing the first sleep I had had in days from my eyes. I looked wildly around and jumped up out of my deck chair. Steady, I admonished myself, steady and strong as the Rock of Gibraltar which was receding in the distance. The fine figure of a man walked by and we nodded to each other, smiling.

He was in his sixties, beautifully dressed, handsome, distinguished, with the proud bearing of a man who had overcome all odds, left no stone unturned, and come out of it with his hands clean. This was the second trip we were taking together on the Algeciras-Tangier run, and the sight of him once more drove me crazy. Who was he? Where had I seen him before? His face was as familiar to me as Harry Truman's or Casey Stengel's. I had seen it in a thousand newspapers, a hundred newsreels. He was someone who meant something to me . . .

I was the first off the ferry, the first through Moroccan customs, and I ran down the line of taxis until I found my friend.

"Mohammed," I said breathlessly.

"Madame," he said sadly. "Oh, madame."

"You have news of my husband?"

"Yes," he said sadly.

"You know where he is!"

"Yes, madame," he said sadly, "yes."

We nodded and smiled at each other, the distinguished gentleman and I. He stopped for a moment and waved his hand across the rail.

"Always an inspiring sight," he said, "the Rock."

"Yes," I said.

"Fifty pesetas for you," I said.

"Gracias, senora."

"And fifty pesetas for you," I said.

"Muchas gracias, senora!"

They went back, with more enthusiasm, to repotting again the plants. I went to the desk to inquire if Tom was still around.

"Inspiring," the distinguished gentleman said, "always inspiring."

"Yes," I said.

He turned away.

"Governor!" I exclaimed. "Ex-Governor Brown!"

He turned back.

"Senator!" I said. "Ex-Senator Brown!"

He smiled, gratified.

"Sir, I'm from Connecticut and you were the finest governor and senator we ever had! I always voted for you!"

"Thank you, my dear."

"Are you on a vacation, Governor Brown, Senator?"

"No, hardly."

"That's right. Nobody from Connecticut would spend their vacation commuting like we are. It's business, of course."

"Yes," Governor-Senator Brown said gravely. "Perhaps the most important of my life. Nice meeting you."

He strode away.

"Ah, madame," Mohammed said sadly.

I stamped my foot.

"Madame is full of dismay."

"No, but there must be a better way to find a husband. Mohammed, that woman at the hotel here, the blonde . . . uh . . . you know . . ."

"She is not nearly so attractive as madame, believe me."

"Thank you. In fact, thank you very much. Do you know amything about her?"

"Very little."

"Perhaps the concierge . . ."

"I have spoken to him. I have all his information."

"Tell me."

"Her name is not Wade."

I nodded knowingly, then smiled encouragingly.

"Her name is Marlene Tiffany. All else I can say is that she lately had a night club in southern Spain, the Chez Marlene et Lorna . . ."

"Where in southern Spain?"

"Torremolinos."

"Thank you, Mohammed."

"I can't hear you, yell louder."

"This is Mrs. Wade . . ."

"Where are you, Mrs. Wade?" Clifford justifiably asked. "Algeciras or Tangier?"

"Tangier at the moment."

"Have you caught up to him?"

"Not quite, Clifford."

"Do you want me to come over? I can drop everything."

"Not yet. How's Gordy?"

"He's behaving very well, Mrs. Wade. I just got him to sleep. He was worried about your not calling at your regular time."

"My ferry was late."

"Do you want to talk to my mother?"

"No, I want to talk to you. When you were in Torremolinos did you know a Marlene Tiffany and a Lorna somebody?"

"Lorna Crowley," Clifford said. "They ran the Chez Marlene et Lorna. I used to do some steering for the joint until I got a better offer from El Whiskey Club. But Marlene and Lorna and me stayed good friends. I did them a big favor when they sold the joint. They were being watched and they couldn't figure how to sneak four million pesetas out of Spain. Four million pesetas in thousand-peseta notes is pretty bulky. So I said nobody ever suspects a drunk and they ought to get some guy drunk and without him knowing it stash pesetas in his coat lining and keep him going back and forth between Tangier and Algeciras until all the pesetas were out of Spain and . . . oh, Mrs. Wade! Mrs. Wade, I'm sorry. You sure you don't want me to come over?"

"No, Clifford, you've done about all that could be expected of a fourteen-year-old. It's time you were in bed."

The ferry from Algeciras came in on time, got moored smoothly, unloaded quickly . . . and there I was left standing on the dock. I had so looked forward to seeing him come staggering down the gangplank, the lining of his corduroy jacket stuffed with thousand peseta notes. Besides being disappointed and worried, I was baffled. The Algeciras Mrs. Wade had been aboard, but not Tom. The meaning of that was obvious. If she left Spain it had to mean that the last of the four million pesetas were safely out of Spain. Tom had made, or was making, his final delivery.

"Mohammed," I said, "is there any other way to get from Algeciras to Tangier?"

"Today is Tuesday?"

"Yes."

"One could have taken a taxi or ferry to Gibraltar, then the plane to Tangier."

"The airport, Mohammed."

"The plane arrived two hours ago."

"The hotel, Mohammed, the shortest way and fast, fast, fast!"

Mohammed made the ten-minute trip in a little less than half an hour, due to being delayed by a policeman who frowned on his going down a one-way street the wrong way

at sixty miles an hour while blowing his horn in a hospital
quiet zone and trying to bilk his fare by not having raised his
flag and set his meter going. Because of me, the lady tourist,
the policeman forgave Mohammed of all his offenses except
the last. He escorted us back to the dock, made Mohammed
put up his flag, and waved us off, pleased that he had been
of so much help to me.

I was rushing across the lobby when I saw it. It was
being carried on a hanger by an Arab boy so small that he
had to hold it head high to keep it from dragging on the
floor.

"Young man," I said, "what are you doing with that coat?"

"Returning it, madame."

"From where?"

"My father's tailor shop, madame. The lining needed re-
pairing."

"Who sent it to be repaired, young man?"

"Mrs. Wade, madame. She and another lady stopped by
with it on their way to the bank."

"Are you returning it to Mrs. Wade?"

"No, madame. To Mr. Wade."

"Allah be praised! Where is Mr. Wade?"

"Mrs. Wade said I would find him in the café, Madame,
having coffee."

"Do you know him to see him?"

"No, madame, but he will be the gentleman without a
coat."

"Thank you and may you have a hundred sons."

I followed him into the café and watched him locate
Tom. He was sitting in a booth. He seemed surprised to
discover that he wasn't wearing a coat. He put it on, tipped
the boy, and sat gently down.

He looked peaked.

I steadied myself, prior to claiming my own. Then I
noticed that Tom was smiling bravely and talking to some-

one I couldn't see. Perhaps I was oversensitive, but I slipped across the café and into the next booth. Maybe there were more Mrs. Wades than you could shake a stick at.

"Wade," a man was saying, "I was recently asked to attend a meeting of the heads of nine or ten of the leading agencies on Madison Avenue. As you may know, I was in the game before entering politics."

"Yes, I do know, Governor," Tom said. "Brighton and Brown."

"Well, now, Wade, it appears that you have spearheaded a movement that threatens to drain the Avenue of more talent than it can afford to lose. Your action has been an unfortunate inspiration to far too many of our best, most creative admen. The latest poll shows that eight men have left to write novels, five to paint, four to be composers, and one is studying acting with Uta Hagen. This dangerous drift must be stopped and the top-level boys feel that if you can be persuaded to come back into the fold, that will do it. I have been commissioned to approach you and, I might add, it's been difficult. Wade, the Avenue is prepared to make you a very attractive offer. In fact, you can choose your own job at your own terms."

"Governor," Tom said, "I wouldn't want to take a step like this without consulting my wife . . . Emmy!"

"Hello, Tom," I said.

"Governor," Tom said, "this is my wife."

"I'll be damned," the ex-governor-senator said.

Chapter Twenty-five

The 6:02 was late, but not much. As I was taking the ice out of the pitcher, I heard Tom's car turn into the drive. I put the ice back in the pitcher, stirred, and poured the martinis. It was unwinding time in Fairfield County.

"Hello, dear."

"Hi, Em."

"Tough day?"

"About usual," Tom said. "Brutal."

"Drink your martini. Bad trip? Air-conditioning break down?"

"Yes, but I made a small slam in clubs. Gordy not home yet?"

"No, it must have gone into extra innings."

"Clifford called me at the office."

"Really?"

"He's on his way to his father in Chicago. He took me to lunch at the Stork Club."

"How is he?"

"Worried about the tariff."

"He'll get that straightened out. Talked to the mailman today."

"How's Charley?"

"Great. His wife was about to resign from the Book-of-the-Month Club until she read Bob Talbot's book."

"Met Sal Mineo at the Stork."

"You met him!"

"Clifford introduced us. Gordy got a ride home?"

"Yes. Al brought your gabardine back today."

"Good."

"And all six shirts. Another martini?"

"Please, this rat race!"

"Golf this weekend or sailing?"

"Golf on Saturday. Sunday I thought Gordy and I would sail the *Emmy* over to Great Length. Any mail?"

"Three Occupants, one Householder and that real estate agent in Martha's Vineyard. His choice listings."

"I thought we might travel this summer. France, Italy, Greece. I get five weeks vacation. Oh, incidentally, I got another raise."

"So soon again?"

"I'm afraid so."

"Can we afford it?"

"The tax man thinks we might. The Utrillo looks good there."

"Better than the Jackson Pollock. Peeling like it is. Another martini?"

"At least, God, this rat race!"

"Dear, look at it this way. Someone has to do it."

"Hi, Mom!" Gordy yelled from the kitchen. "Where's Daddy?"

"Here," I said.